BONY AND THE KELLY GANG

Arthur Upfield was born in England in 1888.
When he was twenty-three he emigrated to
Australia, and during the First World War he
served with the Australian Army. After the
war he roamed Australia, working as a
boundary-rider, offside driver, cattle-drover,
rabbit-trapper, and cattle station manager. He
got to know the Aborigines and their customs,
and this material later appeared in his *Bony*
novels. The half-aboriginal sleuth, Detective
Napoleon Bonaparte, is based on a character
Upfield knew well. Many *Bony* novels have
appeared since the first in 1951, and they have
also formed the basis for a television series.

Arthur Upfield died in 1965.

ARTHUR UPFIELD

BONY AND THE
KELLY GANG

Pan Books Sydney and London
in association with William Heinemann

First published 1960 by William Heinemann Limited
This edition published 1983 by Pan Books (Australia) Pty Limited
68 Moncur Street, Woollahra, New South Wales
in association with William Heinemann Limited

© Arthur W. Upfield 1960
ISBN 0 330 27041 9

Printed and bound in Australia by the Dominion Press Hedges and Bell, Melbourne

CONTENTS

CHAPTER I

Where Foxes Lived with Rabbits

THE SECONDARY road was ruler-straight across the narrow coastal lowlands to the base of the Southern Mountains of New South Wales. It was bituminised, and on either side extended paddocks of grass, green with life and studded with fat cattle. Behind the man walking this road was the highway from Sydney, and beyond it lazed the Pacific. Before him rose tree-covered slopes to support the granite faces of the uplands high to three thousand feet above sea level.

This was certainly not Inspector Bonaparte's country of mulga forest, rolling sand dunes and saltbush plains, of barren residuals and ironstone ridges. This country was no less beautiful, no less mysterious, but it wasn't his own. The faces of the mountains frowned at him.

Superintendent Casement had said, turning from a wall map to his littered desk:

"I remember when I was a small kid on the farm at home, and had to leave for a city boarding-school. The problem was what to do with my three ferrets. The old man couldn't be bothered, and my mother disliked having anything to do with them. The night before I left, I took them to the largest rabbit burrow on the place and let 'em loose, knowing they wouldn't starve for rabbits. And next morning I ran out to say good-bye to them, and found them all dead on the roof of the burrow. You see, I didn't count on foxes living with the rabbits."

Inspector Bonaparte remembered glancing up from his long brown fingers which were rolling a cigarette, and saying:

"And your two-legged ferrets have been found dead on or near a burrow in the Southern Highlands."

"One dead and several badly mangled. The burrow is near

7

this cross I've just made on the map. Perhaps I should say the burrow is *thought* to be near the cross."

Bonaparte recalled lighting the cigarette and being elated by the challenge in the Superintendent's small brown eyes. That was the moment of decision, and he had made it, with complete knowledge of the official data in mind, and all details of that wall map as clear as when he had turned from it to roll his cigarette.

This was certainly not his country, with its wide grass paddocks ending against walls of rock thrown up probably a million years ago. Take an aborigine from this country and put him down in the 'Back of Beyond', and he would die of thirst if he didn't die of fright. Reverse the transfer, and the Outbacker would thrust his head into a wombat hole and howl with cold misery. Everything is relative with the aborigines, even with Detective Inspector Napoleon Bonaparte, now travelling under the name of Nathaniel Bonnay.

Now and then a car overtook him, but he made no effort to thumb a ride. He was waiting for a truck bearing the registration plates 101-PXA, and knew that somewhere behind it a police car would be keeping discreetly out of the driver's rear-vision mirror. Travelling by truck to the suspected burrow would be preferable to walking all the way, and even when he did reach it there were sporting odds that it would house no foxes.

Much preparation had been done prior to putting Nat Bonnay on this road to the Southern Highlands, and much detailed work had gone into the plan to introduce him to Cork Valley where its people had long been suspected of unlawful activities. Superintendent Casement's allegorical rabbit burrow was probably no larger than a six-room house, but the Cork Valley locale was something like four square miles in area.

It was now early April; the sun was pleasantly warm and the maples and other ornamental trees about the occasional homestead were beginning to be coloured by autumn. The usually nattily dressed Inspector Bonaparte was walking with a loping spring, but nothing else remained of him in the

8

character of Nat Bonnay. His clothes were old and far from neat. His boots were elastic-sided riding boots. His trousers were of rough gaberdine, tight about the thighs and full in the seat. The jacket was made of a cheaper cloth, and the blue shirt collar was frayed slightly and dirty. He carried a small battered suitcase, and with his felt hat he waved away the occasional fly.

The truck crept up behind him like a stalking fox, and Bony sprang guiltily back when he saw it two hundred yards behind him. He started to run off the road, stopped indecisively, turned as though seeking cover, finally stood and raised a hand for a lift.

It was a three-ton truck, with gleaming bumper bars and newly painted red cabin. The driver slowed down slightly, then accelerated as though he didn't like the look of the wayfarer. But he stopped the truck fifty yards on, obviously still uneasy in his mind when Bony settled himself on the seat beside him.

Neither spoke for sixty seconds. During this time the truck driver became conscious of the other's interest in his rear-vision mirror.

"Thanks," said the wayfarer. "Good sort of day."

"Last of the summer," agreed the driver. "Where are you headed?"

"Nowhere in particular so long's it's away from Sydney. How far are you going?"

"I turn off into the hills twenty miles this side of Bowral. What's wrong with Sydney?"

The fingers of Bony's left hand drummed on the suitcase resting on his knees. The sign of nervousness was not lost on the driver who waited for the answer.

"Plenty," admitted the wayfarer. "Sydney's getting too cold to sleep out in. Besides"—he permitted the drone of the vehicle to drown out his voice before adding—"I'm not popular in Sydney." The farms and the colourful farm homesteads drifted past, but the granite faces of the uplands remained distantly aloof. "Bowral! What sort of place is it? Big or small?"

"Smallish. Four-pub town. Three policemen. Five hundred yapping dogs."

"Oh!" The traveller appeared to be shocked by the information. The driver waited for the shock to subside, and, with an elbow, assured himself that the spare tyre lever was positioned in the door pocket and available for instant use. The traveller said: "I've no money for the pubs, and no time for the cops. I did hear there was spud digging out this way. And dairy farms and such."

"That's so."

The front of the great range revealed a dent, and soon the dent became a bay and the wings of the bay came out to meet and take the truck as though it were a ship seeking shelter. Now the bare rock cliffs towered high above the precipitous tree-armoured slopes.

"You were saying?" prompted the driver.

"That I wouldn't mind taking a job."

"So you did. And something about not being popular with the police. Trouble behind you?"

"Trouble behind me. Where I want it to stay."

"Don't we all."

The truck slid round a bend and buried its nose in a mountain. Thereafter the bends were many and sharp, and the engine growled as it dragged the vehicle up the steep gradient skirted by the great gums and the lesser scrub so envious of their height. Now at a greatly reduced speed, the driver had time to talk, and his quiet voice, devoid of noticeable accent, hadn't to be raised.

"I have troubles, too. Taxes, Death and Damnation. I've a patch of spuds itching to be lifted to a good market. We're isolated somewhat. No pub nearer than Bowral, and no policeman. Still, we live pretty comfortable. What kind of trouble are you aiming to keep behind you?"

Bony slowly rolled a cigarette, hesitating to provide personal information. He glanced beyond the window, through a break in the forest trees to the breathtaking vista of space built over the lowlands. Having lit the cigarette, he glanced the other way at the driver, noting again the rough, but good, working suit indicative of the farmer-employer, and the voice quiet without accent. He was well under fifty, of medium height and weight. His eyes were dark and his hair almost as black as Bony's. Bony's hair was straight and slicked down, the driver's hair was curly and thick.

"Trouble behind me could be my business," Bony said, easily. "But that plot of spuds waiting to be lifted . . . Well, my main trouble's two years behind me. Did time for a horse deal, but the police don't choose to forget it. Couple of weeks back, came down to Sydney to spend a bit of a cheque. Went broke. Had to sleep in the Domain. Got to be recognised, and told to get out of town, or else. No money. So walked out. As I said, there could be something in that spud lifting."

"Main trouble!" echoed the driver. "What's the lesser?"

"Tossed into my lap. Last night I camped just off the highway. A hobo saw my fire and camped with me. He had a chook; I had a fire. We grilled the chook, and the hobo was careful to burn all the feathers. He told me about this road and where it went, and all that. Then he told me he'd pinched the chook, and suggested we could pinch another for breakfast. I sweated a bit until I got away from him. I've pinched a horse or two, but I'm not aiming to be taken for pinching a fowl. Get jugged for lifting one fowl, and the police'll make it twenty fowls."

"Any difference between horses and fowls?" asked the driver, laughingly.

"Different weights for one thing. Different values, too. Besides, I didn't pinch the chook, and didn't know it was pinched until half of it was inside me."

"But you had the goods on you, or rather in you. Where did the hobo steal the fowl?"

A casual question. A question expected and the answer provided.

"I wasn't that interested. He told me he was making south, and so he must have lifted the bird up towards Wollongong. The police don't have different values. All the same to them if it's a horse or a fowl or an elephant."

"Huh! How many horses set against the elephant?"

"Three. Cost me two years, less remissions. Need we talk about it? You have spuds to lift, not horses. And, I'll tell you again, chooks aren't in my line."

Miniature waterfalls came sliding down from the heights, to slip across the road and begin again as waterfalls. The country was a paradise of green growth, of up-and-down land slopes, of sparkling, leaping water, of bitumen roads and wheel traffic.

At one sharp bend there was a turn-off track, and here the driver stopped his truck and switched off the ignition. The heated engine sighed, and silently the driver leaned forward to take tobacco and papers from the dash cupboard.

"What's your name?" he asked.

"Bonnay. Nat Bonnay."

"Tell me more, Nat; where you come from, and why you don't make back to where you come from."

"Easy, though I can't see it's your business. Actually, I'm a Queenslander, and I came south to work on a property out from Tenterfield. The boss thinks he can breed racehorses and train 'em. You being so interested, his name is Marsdon. I got three of his year-old fillies fourteen miles out of his back paddock and into a horse float between sundown and sun-up. The feller with the float took them ninety miles that day to his place, and when he's taking them out of the float, a police-man rides up and says: 'Ha!' Where we slipped, I don't know, but we got two years each. When I was inside, the wife goes to live with her folk, and they threaten to shoot me if I ever turn up there. Now d'you think we could forget it and talk about spuds?"

The driver switched on the ignition and started the truck up the less steep grade of the side track and Bony was pleased that so far the deep-laid plan evolved by Superintendent casement was proceeding well.

Eventually the truck gained the table-top of a wide and open ridge and here was a white-painted house. The situation was ideal. Behind the house grew tall ironbarks which provided shelter from the cold westerlies of winter, and no matter how the southerlies blew, it would be cosily protected within the semi-vacuum provided by the cliff faces fronting over the coastal lowlands.

"My mother lives here with a brother of mine," the driver told Bony. "Brother was tossed off a motor bike years ago, and never walked since. I have some stuff to deliver. You stay here. I'll talk to him about the spuds."

He stopped the truck at the gate in the white-painted picket fence, and from the rear took a case which he carried to the house verandah. On the verandah was a bed, and propped up with pillows was a man with unruly iron-grey hair. Beside the bed, and within reach of his hands stood a large telescope on a tripod, and through this glass he could watch ships passing at sea, and gaze into the great bowl of the valley on the far side of the ridge. It was down there that Superintendent Casement thought his rabbit burrow might be.

A small woman came from the house to join in the conversation. Hens strutted outside the fence. Blue smoke rose from one of the two chimneys, and kookaburras blasted the quiet scene with guffaws of satanic laughter. A moment or two later, the driver beckoned to Bony.

Standing at the foot of the bed, Bony immediately saw that these three people were related. The bed-ridden man was older than the truck driver. Despite his immobility, his complexion was weathered, due to the fact that he lived always on this open verandah, his only protection being the movable screens. For a long moment he gazed at Nat Bonnay, eyes hard and brilliant, and when he spoke his voice was low and pleasant.

"There's a job for you down in the valley," he said. "We're peaceful in these parts. You lift the spuds, and you live peaceful, and you'll be looked after and paid good rates. As long as you don't claim to come from Ulster you won't have a war on your hands."

A humorous quirk appeared at the corners of his mouth, and brought a smile to Bony's eyes when the latter asked:

"Think I could claim to come from Northern Ireland?"

"Where could your father claim to come from?"

"I don't know. My mother never told, that I recall."

"Like that, eh!"

"Like that. Any harm in saying he might have come out from County Mayo?"

Both men chuckled, and the invalid said:

"Better stick to the truth, perhaps. All right, Nat. The job's yours."

CHAPTER 2

Snugly in Cork Valley

THE TRACK from the white house crossed level ground for five hundred yards, passed over a rough but well constructed wooden bridge spanning a gully, and proceeded down steep gradients skirting the inner slopes of the coastal mountains. Until the bridge was reached the traveller wouldn't expect to be so rewarded by the colourful space which rested like a halo on Cork Valley.

The white house stood on the rim of a great amphitheatre. The floor was sea-green in the light of the westering sun, and pale blue where the shadows lay. Against the southern wall a brilliant silver streak marked the eternal fall of water, and near its base the tiny houses were white squares. To the right of the settlement, and separated from it by green paddocks, stood a mansion of many chimneys and windows which at this time of day were glaring searchlights, as though directed suspiciously at the descending truck.

The driver had to brake all the way, and keep the engine in low gear. The track was the original entrance to Cork Valley, its surface rough, yet maintained by expert draining, and at every inner bend of the mountain folds was another bushman-built bridge. It was obvious that no public money had ever been spent on the road or bridges.

Bony was aware from Superintendent Casement's map that this was the front door to Cork Valley, as he was aware there were no known back or side entrances. So far the plan to introduce him as Nat Bonnay was proceeding smoothly, and the long-held suspicions of the people at Cork Valley were being confirmed. Having announced himself as a thief and a thief's associate, he was still offered work and, presumably, protection from the police.

As Bonnay, he did not know the name of the truck driver,

or the people at the house on the rim. He had not been informed, and in his assumed character he would be expected to ask, otherwise it would be presumed that he knew, and how could he explain knowing names when he ought not to know them. A small point, but one powerful enough to slay a ferret. Casually he said:

"Who am I working for?"

"The name's Mike Conway. I'm the Cork Valley carrier and storekeeper. My wife is the post-mistress. All right with you?"

"What d'you mean: all right with me?" Bony retorted. "I got a right to know who I'm working for, haven't I?"

"Yes, you have that," admitted the driver. "Why the heat?"

"Blast it! You asked me if it's all right with me to know. Why shouldn't I know?"

"No answer, Nat, no answer," came the quietly spoken words. "You go to a good school?"

"Why the hell not?" Bony almost snarled. "Think because my mother was an aborigine I'm a sort of wild animal? 'Course I went to school. I passed my Intermediate. Then what? Back to the land. Anyway, what d'you want me to do? Dig spuds or teach at school?"

"Pipe down, Nat, pipe down. I didn't mean to rile you." Bony continued to sit half turned to the driver. "Life is what you get out of it, not what it likes to give you, I'm going to pay you seven bob a bag to lift spuds, and the wife will charge you three pounds a week for board and keep. And when the crop's lifted, there's other work you can do if you care to stay on."

"Expect I'll be staying. The Valley looks good to me," conceded Bony.

"Good on you. Winter can be cold, and there's plenty of fogs, but the quarters are snug enough. And another thing, Nat, us Conways and the Kellys don't stand for foreign interference. Get it?"

"Bit by bit, Mike. We'll get along."

"Sure we will. It's a deal?"

"Well, I'm not walking back, and I'm liking that word 'snug'."

Fifteen minutes later and five hundred feet lower, the offside front tyre blew out, and the driver had to proceed on a flat to the next inside bend and relax the vehicle against the bank. The new man evidently knew what to do; he disengaged the spare from its rack and had it ready for Conway before the wheel was jacked. The change occupied them twenty minutes.

"You aren't exactly useless," commented the driver when they were moving again. "Two miles to go, and then a cup of tea."

"That inner tube could be chewed to ribbons," surmised Bony, thoughtfully adding the twenty minutes occupied by the change to the twenty odd minutes spent at the white house. Forty minutes might cause a bad hitch in a time-table.

"Could be so," was the cheerful agreement. "Still it'll come off the income tax."

"The skin off my hands digging spuds won't come off my tax," complained Bony.

"Don't worry, Nat. You'll be paid in hard cash."

The next bridge they came to crossed a gully which looked a mile deep. It was narrow and had no side walls or rails, and the man accustomed to the level square miles of the inland shrank back. Soon afterwards they arrived at the valley bed, and here the track was better as it wound over low bald hills on which cattle grazed in knee-high grass.

Cork Valley! There was not a valley like this in County Cork, Ireland. The man known to all his friends as Bony, and now in Cork Valley as Nat Bonnay, a horse thief and partaker of stolen fowls, was entranced by its beauty: the autumnal tints; the soft blues of the shadows and the jet black gaping jaws of the surrounding mountain slopes and cliffs. From a rise he saw the houses of Cork Valley, pure white against the green wall of trees divided by the living silver of a high waterfall.

They approached the settlement. Bony counted seven houses: three on one side and four on the other of a wide unmade street. Beyond the houses stood a large shed-like building he guessed to be a dairy and creamery, and as they drew near he noted people gathering in the short street, and Mike Conway exclaimed:

"What the hell's up now!"

The first house on the left was combined with the general store, and just beyond the store was what might be a garage. At this building Conway stopped the truck, and it was instantly surrounded by half a dozen men who offered no sign either of welcome or hostility. A huge man, with flame-red hair, small, intensely blue eyes, and a full beard as thick and as red as his hair, jerked open the door of the truck.

"Come on, you," he ordered, the need for haste plain in voice and eyes.

Bony lowered himself from the high cabin, dragging his old suitcase with him. He was seized by two men and urged, with no possibility of successful resistance, off the street and into the garage-like building. It contained farm equipment, and stacks of potatoes and pie melons. At the far end a grinning boy held up a trap door in the floor. The man with the great red beard said:

"Down quick, me lad. The police are right on your tail."

Wooden steps descended to a cellar. A hurricane lamp burned on a small table. There was a bed bearing a small pile of folded blankets. He sat on the chair beside the table, and laughed silently as he rolled a cigarette.

His underground room was nine by nine feet, and the ceiling, the floor of the shed above, was not more than seven feet high. It smelled fresh and dry, and there was a bed and table and chair offering mute proof that he wasn't the first occupant.

The twenty minutes' delay due to the blow-out had almost wrecked the plan to introduce Inspector Bonaparte into Cork Valley. Had the pursuing police caught up with him they would have had to arrest him, and to arrest him was not the purpose of the pursuit. They merely wanted to confirm his story.

Bony could hear the murmur of voices, and presently he heard an approaching car. He mounted the steps to bring his ear close to the shed floor, and he heard the car arrive, its engine stopped, the doors slammed shut. He ventured to raise the trap an inch, and heard clearly the conversation outside the open-fronted shed. Sergeant O'Leary, of Wollongong, was saying:

"We are looking for a feller calling himself Bonnay. He's got a record, and we believe he's concerned with thefts on the outskirts of Wollongong. He was last seen at the turn-off from the Hume Highway, and a couple of blackberry-pickers at the foot of the pass think he was in your truck."

"That's so, Sarge," came the quiet even voice of Mike Conway. "Half abo, I think. I picked him up a couple of miles in from the Highway. Said he was making for Bowral way and he asked me if there was any work going over there. What's he done?"

"No matter," growled the sergeant. "Exceptin' he's got a record as long as your arm. You bring him here?"

"No. Not in the habit of bringing waifs and strays to Cork Valley. I put him down at the turn-off on the mountain road. You call on my brother?"

"Your brother said he didn't notice him with you." Sergeant O'Leary's voice was distinctly chilly. "You haven't unloaded yet, I see."

"What of it?" softly asked Conway.

"Well, get along. Unload. The feller might have hopped up into the load as you moved off from the mountain road."

"Unload yourself," a man shouted, and Bony thought he must be the red-headed giant.

"That'll do you, Red Kelly," snapped the sergeant, and again the quiet tones of Conway reached the enthralled Bony.

"Cut it out, Red. Give us a hand, you fellers, to unload for the sergeant. Wire into the shed, cased stuff into the store."

Through the chink between the floor and the trap, Bony could see the activity outside. A man came into the shed rolling fencing wire, and Bony closed the trap and climbed down the steps. The wire was placed on the trap, and a moment later another coil was stacked on top of the first. Up the steps once again, Bony listened and heard some of the conversation above.

"Have a look behind those stacked spuds, constable," a man said, giving a deep chuckle. "The feller could be among 'em." Another man added: "Give it a go, constable. Them aborigines are slippery bastards. What about trying the rafters?"

Another coil of wire was dropped on the stack over the trap door, and then sounds of activity abated, and the voices became distant and the words blurred. Bony descended again to sit on the chair beside the table and roll another cigarette, complacently satisfied that the plan had succeeded in its dual purpose.

The story he had told Conway of being imprisoned for stealing horses, and associating with a fowl-stealing hobo was now substantiated by the police. It was proved that he was a person of ill repute. And further, it was now proved that these Cork Valley people weren't above harbouring a wanted man, and the suspicion was strengthened that they had been closely associated with crimes for several years. They were an anachronism in an orderly country. They owned this rich land pocket amid mountains extending south of Sydney to the Alps, and farther still into the mountainous maze of Gippsland having its western extremity but a few miles north of Melbourne. And on one side of the Highlands the rich coastal belt and on the other the farms and grazing properties and thriving towns and railways.

Superintendent Casement's analogical rabbit burrow included a region much larger than Cork Valley. The dead and mangled ferrets had not been found in Cork Valley itself but miles from it, and no member of the community had been charged with a serious crime for the past forty years.

"They're a stubborn crowd, Bony, and mighty cunning," he had explained. "Try to evade paying licence fees for anything, just for the hell of it. Fought and beat the Education Department about sending the children to school by bus outside the Valley. Now they run their own school. Customs people are convinced they've operated stills for many years but could never locate one. Farmers right outside the area have repeatedly lost cattle and horses, and shortly before petrol rationing was terminated, a semi-trailer truck broke down on the pass up the mountains, and, when the driver was away telephoning for assistance, fifty forty-gallon drums of juice disappeared.

"Seven years ago, a party of Customs investigators made a

raid and when returning, their car fell through a bridge. Cork Valley never pays rates until compelled to, so the road in doesn't concern the local council. We sent in a man last year. Went in as a potato digger. Two weeks later they delivered him at the Bowral Hospital, swearing he'd started a brawl. He couldn't admit he was police, and he couldn't prove the brawl was staged for his benefit. Nine years ago the body of a man was found in a tidal creek south of Kiama. Never identified. Dentures found in a pocket didn't fit his mouth. Nothing to prove that he was murdered by anyone at Cork Valley. But back of the creek are the mountains and in the mountains is Cork Valley.

"This recent crime is nearer Cork Valley, and the victim was an excise officer of the Customs Department. On December 21 last year the body of a man was found on the road three miles from Bowral by a milk-collecting truck driver. Road marks as well as the condition of the body pointed to a hit-and-run affair, but the pathologist's report says that the man had been dead for several hours before being deliberately run over.

"The body was dressed in worn working clothes and boots, but the hands proved he wasn't a working man. It has taken us four months to identify him, and that because of unusual circumstances.

"Excise Officer Eric Torby was granted three months' leave, as from the beginning of December; was single, no relatives, lived in lodgings in Sydney. Told his landlady he was going bushwalking in the Southern Highlands, and anticipated being away for weeks. She states he left wearing plus-fours and a tweed coat, and carried in his rucksack extra underwear. Says further, that he was interested in geology, and took with him a geologist's hammer. Cork Valley would interest a geologist, Bony?"

"And a still would interest an excise officer," Bony had said. "I'll study that wall map again, and we'll think up a plan to get me into Cork Valley."

The opening phase of the plan had succeeded, and Inspector Bonaparte, alias Nathaniel Bonnay, now listened to the departure of the police car. The ensuing silence continued for half an hour, when he heard the sound of rolls of wire being removed from the trap door.

The trap was raised and down the steps came Mike Conway and the huge red-bearded man called Kelly. Conway sat on the bed and fingered the old suitcase. Redbeard stood with fists clamped to his hips and stared down at the seated Bony.

CHAPTER 3

Dinner with the Family

"So you're on the run eh? Stealing horses and thieving a poor widder-woman's fowls." In the lamplight the big man's eyes were almost black, and Bony remembered them to be fiercely blue. "If you would be after stealin' fowls at Cork Valley, or borrowing a horse or two, be carshous."

"I didn't rob the widow although I ate her chook," Bony particularised. "The horses I took belonged to a squatter."

Red Kelly made the first of his many mistakes, saying:

"Stand up when you speak to an Irish gintleman."

Bony stood; and Red Kelly observed the metamorphosis Bony could achieve. The slightly drooping, shifty-eyed descendant of two races became a blazing-eyed spitting panther as he took the three steps necessary to stand chest to chest with the man a foot taller and a foot wider than himself.

"Are you a squatter to give me orders?" he shouted. "Are you a rubber-necked warder, having been in gaol yourself and knowing their ways?"

"Now now, me lad, now now," soothed Red Kelly, a grin beginning to part the red whiskers. His great head nodded with approbation. "You'll do, Nat. Got to be sure. Got to check. Mike here wants his spuds lifted. You want to lift 'em. After that there's work and good livin' for them as likes both to come at the same time."

Bony nonchalantly strode back to his chair. The two men watched the fire in him die out, both a little startled by the unexpected outburst. Conway said, in his quiet voice:

"We just want to be sure you're not a no-hoper, Nat. That's all. You don't mind us checking, now, do you?"

"Go ahead."

"Open your case, Nat."

"You open it. It's beside you."

They examined every article from a spare shirt to a new hairbrush and comb. They were interested in a stockwhip and a pair of worn spurs with rowels of twin sixpences to make the ring. They glanced at each other when one passed over the kangaroo-hide riding-boots.

"If you're looking for proof that I'm not the premier of New South Wales, take a looksee through this," Bony said, tossing his wallet beside the oddments emptied on the bed.

"If you were even related to that renegade I'd ring your neck," snarled Red Kelly. He withdrew the papers from the wallet: a soiled driver's licence bearing the name Nathaniel Bonnay, a letter addressed to 'Dear Nat' bearing a Tenterfield address, asking for money, and signed 'Your Old Father', and a Parole Card bearing Bonnay's name and particulars.

The big man returned the papers, sighed, tossed the wallet back to Bony.

"Clean, Mike. Take him on."

"I intended to," Mike Conway said, and Redbeard came back with:

"I know you did, but it's me being carshous what's kept the peace in Cork Valley." He turned to Bony. "All right, Nat. We'll see how you shape. We'll be startin' off on that foot, and you can call me Red. Every blessed soul here calls me that to me face."

He mounted the steps to the shed above, and Conway asked: "These quarters suit you, Nat?"

"Why not? Dry and . . . and snug, as just now proved."

"That was the police. Right on your tailboard. Seemed anxious about you." In view of his declared occupation and his clothes, Conway's enunciation could be ascribed only to an education at a church school. Low in tone, his voice was always soft and seldom betrayed emotion, but in him were depths which Bony could sense, and even now his judgment of the new hand was delayed.

"I could hear, even when the trap was closed down," Bony admitted, and again gave evidence of the assumed trait of touchiness by asking: "You getting nervous about me?"

"Not yet, Nat." Conway smiled. "Hungry men are prone to temper. Come on up and have a wash and meet the family at dinner."

He led the way up the steps. Bony now took stock of the world above floorboards. Outside the open fronted store shed the unmade 'street' was deserted. The sun had set, and all the northern sky was green where it rested on the rim of the great amphitheatre. Red Kelly rode at a gallop down the road towards the waterfall, and Bony saw him turn off to enter a wall of scrub connecting the end house with the factory building beyond. Obviously he was returning to the large stone mansion of the many windows which stood boldly against the wall of mountain covering its rear.

Bony was taken to the laundry behind the general store-cum-residence occupied by Mike Conway and his family, where he was provided with a clean towel and given hot water and soap. Conway washed at another basin, slicked his dark hair with water, and didn't fail to note that Nat Bonnay produced a comb from a pocket and gave his own hair particular attention. This new man was no slouch.

The Conways' large kitchen-living-room surprised Bony. In one wall there were two fireplaces, one an open hearth and the other occupied by a large cooking range. Electric light streamed upon the white cloth, covering a large dining-table with massive legs, and a grandfather clock, at least two hundred years old judging by its carved ornamentation. There were three huge paintings in heavy gilt frames, and cedarwood cabinets flanked by chairs of such an antiquity and exquisite carving that a dealer would dance with envy.

"New man, Mate," Conway said to his wife who turned from the cooking range at their entry. "The name is Nat." She was tall and angular, with the imprint of Ireland on her face, and the soul of Ireland looked shyly from the depth of her large brown eyes. She contented herself by nodding, and turned again to the range.

"Who's that, did you say, Mike?"

The voice came from the high-back chair set before the leaping open fire, and Conway nodded to Bony to follow him

25

and be presented to a tiny woman wearing a white lace cap, a high-necked black bodice and white lace cuffs about her wrists.

"Nat Bonnay, Grandma," replied Mike Conway. "He's going to lift the tatees."

The flames rouged the round face and banished the wrinkles. The flames quickened the dark eyes, and the diamonds in the rings on the doll-like hands lying on the black cloth of her lap returned the flames about the logs.

"So you be taking Nat on to dig the tatees," she said, snappily. "And what will you be paying him, Mike?"

The brogue was unmistakable, and when her grandson spoke it was in his voice, too.

"Seven shillings a bag, Grandma. That's the price these days."

"Just as well the market price is forty pounds a ton, or 'tis ruined we'd all be." The old woman studied Bony, and Bony resisted the habit of bowing slightly. He could detect only curiosity. "What else can you do, Nat Bonnay?"

"I can ride, and muster cattle. I can mend a fence. I'm not very good at it, but I could shoe a horse."

"And steal one," added Conway, chuckling.

"So 'twas told to me," admitted the old woman. "You seem well set up. Can you throw a boomerang, now?"

Bony was conscious of other people behind him, filling the space so evident when he entered the room. The woman in the high back chair knew how to wait, and the throng behind him knew how to wait, too.

"I think I could," he said. "Haven't thrown one for years. I used to be able to play a tune on a gum leaf."

"A musician eh!" chortled the old woman, her eyes and her voice showing that she was needling him.

"Mike!" called Mrs Conway. "Dinner's on the table."

Bony smiled into the dark eyes of Mike's grandmother and turned to the table where several men, women and children of differing years were gathering. He was told to occupy the place at the far end. Mike wheeled the high back chair on its castors to the place set on his right, and sat at one end of the great table with his back to the open hearth. When his wife sat on his left, he gave thanks.

That was a surprise following surprises, and more were to follow. The plates were piled with food, little mountains of potatoes and sprouts next to an alp of curried meat capped with snowy rice. Then he noted that they were not plates but platters. His eyes roamed over dishes of butter and cheese, jugs of cream, jars of pickled onions and bottles of sauces. His attention was then captivated by the diners; there were eleven people at table in addition to Conway and his wife and grandmother.

On his right was the boy who had held up the trap for him. Beyond him was an older boy, and beyond him sat a man who was completely bald and had a face like the proverbial Irishman depicted in Punch. To his left was a girl who immediately captured his romantic heart. She ate quietly, keeping her gaze on her platter. She had dark hair, and even without makeup her face was vivid and wildly beautiful. Two men and two women, with children all older than Bony's immediate neighbour, completed the company.

The meal proceeded in uncommon silence, the adults seldom speaking and the children not at all. Everyone was overtly interested in the new man, and once it was apparent that old Mrs Conway was discussing him with her grandson.

In character with the shy, police-hunted, horse-stealing half-aborigine, Bony at last politely arranged his knife and fork on his empty platter, and sat back in his chair. He waited to be spoken to, and no one did. One by one other diners finished the course, and the girl on his left rose to gather the platters and carry them to the bench. The paintings caught his attention. The room, large though it was, was too small a setting for them. One was of a castle beneath the black draperies of lowering clouds, and was surely the home of the original Dracula. Another was a battle scene, and the third portrayed a man and a woman in the costume of a century long past. The man reminded Bony of the red giant called Red Kelly.

A large plate loaded with apricot pie was set before him, and he smiled his thanks at the girl who served him, his left-hand neighbour. She gave no answering smile, her expression being slightly bored, but after she had again occupied her chair and was eating, he found her looking at him when her face was tilted downward over her spoon and fork. He noted a sustained and furtive interest.

The final course was cheese, bread and butter, and the children were given glasses of water. Bony hoped for some tea or coffee, as without one or the other no Australian meal could be ably digested. When the children, whose ages ranged from ten to about fifteen, departed one after the other, he despaired.

The women rose, and left the room, leaving only the very old dame and the men. The men began to fill pipes or roll cigarettes, and when his pipe was working, the hairless one joined Bony and so banished his feeling of being in a desert. He said, easily:

"I did hear you could throw a boomerang. Never did I see it. Somewhere about there's an old one as long as a cutlass. Would you throw it some time?"

"If it's a large one, it would be for ceremonial use," Bony explained. "Those made for throwing are much smaller."

"There's a book which says the aborigines throw them to knock birds down. Would that be the kind?"

The dark grey eyes were serious, but deep in them natural humour gleamed like sand grains seen through clear mountain water.

"If the birds are close enough," agreed Bony. "Hit or miss, you know. Always chancy. Actually, the abos throw them for amusement."

He was enlarging on the subject and the bald man was engrossed, when Mike Conway set before each two china cups, one containing black coffee and the other a whitish liquid which might have been *kümmel*. Baldhead watched Conway until he was again seated, and broke off in the middle of a question. When the old woman and the others lifted the cups of white liquid, he did likewise. So did Bony.

Mike Conway said: "The Kellys."

The contents of the cups were tossed down throats and the cups of coffee taken up and sipped. Bony was running a little late. He lifted the right cup and tossed the contents down his throat. It must have splashed the sides for his head exploded and his breathing stopped. Fire streaked before his eyes, and water drowned the fire. Beyond his clouded vision he saw Grandma Conway shrieking with mirth. Fighting for air, he staggered to his feet, and someone banged him on the back with a sledge hammer. Baldhead was saying, soothingly:

"Should have warned you, Nat. You take it fast, or you take it extra slow. You never fumble it."

CHAPTER 4

The Spud Digger

INSPECTOR Bonaparte dug 'spuds' in the most beautiful valley in Australia.

Conway's potato crop occupied the crown of a low plateau in the centre of what comprised about three thousand acres of cleared rich land, bordered by broken country massed with trees and surrounded by steep mountain slopes crowned with rock faces. From where he worked he could see the mark of the track slanting down the slopes from Conway's brother's house to cross the valley to the settlement. Behind the settlement, the fall of water dropped from ledge to ledge and was sometimes golden, sometimes blue, and sometimes amber, according to the angle of the sun. Early and late, it was polished pewter.

The big house stood on the far side of the valley and in the morning the slate roof gleamed beneath the sun and at evening the windows reflected the sunlight and could be counted. For Australia it was a mighty house, the transplantation of memory of one in the old country, and there lived Patrick (Red) Kelly, the descendent of the first Kelly who found Cork Valley and settled there.

In that year there had been no railways out from Sydney, and the track from Sydney to Melbourne Town was barely defined by the pioneers' bullock drays. It was the hunting-ground of Starlight and bushrangers of his stamp.

Legend has it that the original Kellys had two children, a boy and a girl. The boy Sean eventually sought a wife, and one day rode up from the valley. A week later he rode into the valley with a woman behind him, whom he claimed, he had captured on the track to Melbourne, and had been married to her by a priest travelling with her party. The sister Nora came of age to seek a husband, and she copied her brother by riding forth from Cork Valley. On returning she was accompanied by two priests and a notorious gentleman of the road known as Black Daniel, with horse pistols stuck in his belt, a beard shaped like a spade, and the price of a hundred guineas on his head. The poor fellow thought he was tough. He must have been comatose from the eyebrows upward, because he thought he was bringing home Nora Kelly to do a trade with her father. How the priests came to be of the party isn't on record. However, they were present when negotiations for ransom were opened with Nora's father and brother.

It is said that Black Daniel had the drop on everyone, his mind occupied with gold, and forgetful of the demure female, victim of his avarice, who was standing with him, her eyes downcast and hands clasped in anxiety. Then something fell on him; one of Nora's heavy boots, it is said; and on returning from unconsciousness he found himself being married to her by one priest, with the other holding him up on his feet. It was then learned that his name was Conway.

Shortly after the demise of the original Kelly, Sean Kelly and Black Daniel Conway feuded over the division of the land. They met early one morning, and when Sean fell mortally wounded he had strength enough to pull a trigger and drop Conway dead in his boots. Following the double funeral, the widows voted to continue the feud, but the wife of the original Kelly came up with his will under the terms of which she inherited all of Cork Valley. She succinctly remarked: "Peace or else."

The aged widow must have been as remarkable a character as her husband. She sent out for a priest-lawyer, and one month after the double funeral, he arrived to say Mass, and afterwards conveyed the conditions of peace to the young widows. A wall was to be built across Cork Valley; one half would be bequeathed to Nora Conway, and the other to her sister-in-law. Young Mrs Kelly was to have that portion on which the great house stood, and Nora Conway was to build her home on the other portion.

The priest-lawyer, a truly saintly man named Cahill, supervised the erection of the stone wall, and saw to it that the legalities were duly executed. Old Mrs Conway now living in the modern settlement, was the granddaughter of Black Daniel Conway, the bushranger, and Nora Kelly who first bashed him and then married him while his knees sagged. Sections of the wall still stood, other sections littered the ground and were replaced with posts and rails. Bony sat with his back to it now and ate his lunch. The sun was warm. The air was crystal clear. The sweetness of this God's garden was ever to remain in his memory.

It seemed that he was the only one who did any real work. Now at the end of the first week his back muscles had firmed and he was liking the labour of digging potatoes, and taking pleasure in counting the bags he filled. There were, of course, hundreds of cows to be milked. The Conways owned power-driven milking-sheds and a cream and cheese factory, electric power being brought in from outside.

Bony became one of the Conway family. He was given breakfast at seven, provided with a lunch bag and billy can for tea, and returned to his underground lodging in time for dinner at six. The soft-spoken Mike Conway treated him with consideration, and the bald-headed Joe Flanagan offered limitless conversation. Flanagan seemed to be the settlement's electrician. The dark Irish beauty, Rosalie Conway, taught at the school and maintained her distance even with her relatives. Sometimes old Mrs Conway impishly delighted in needling the potato digger, and covertly watched at the close of dinner to see if the new man fumbled his Mountain Dew.

Ever careful to act the character of the horse thief lying 'doggo', and ever grateful to the Conways for the opportunity of so doing, Bony made no attempt to climb the social barrier, and made no advances to others of the clan living in the remaining settlement houses. He found himself liking these Conways, for their behaviour in their own home was exemplary. Electrician Flanagan was probably a boarder or a relation. Illegal practices were indeed hard to associate with them.

The first doubt was born at the end of this first week.

He was called to dinner by a small boy who must have been over-eager to perform the chore because on entering the large living-room the table was only then being prepared for the meal. The ancient Mrs Conway, seeing him standing uncertainly just inside the doorway, raised a delicate white finger and beckoned.

Obeying the command, he stood before her where she sat in her high-backed chair at the open fire. She said something in what he presumed to be Gaelic, and waited for his response. Her granddaughter-in-law, turning from the dining-table, spoke a trifle sharply.

"Talk English, Grandma, if you must talk."

"Mind your own business, girl," retorted Grandma. To Bony she repeated: "I said, young man, you could work faster at the tatees. I've been watching you through my spy-glass. I can see you from my window."

"Nat can work as he likes," remarked Mike Conway who had appeared without being noticed. "He's working contract."

"To be sure, he is," agreed the old lady. "But the faster he works the more money he earns. I know what I'm talking about."

There sat a woman who had lived for more than ninety years. She was a relic from an era when only faith and frugality could conquer in the battle with a hard land, and when the ability to laugh was the only ally. Bony could understand her, and perhaps, of all those in Cork Valley, he was the only man who did. Smiling down at her, he watched the swift change in her eyes, and ventured to relax the front he had shown as the hired man.

"I'm thinkin' it's you who is missing out, Mrs Conway," he said with a dreadful imitation of a stage Irishman's brogue. "You see, marm, 'tis like this. The faster I work the quicker I earn me money, as you was just sayin', but the sooner I finish me contract the sooner me eyes will starve from no longer lookin' at a handsome woman."

The old lady tossed her white-capped head and chuckled with glee.

"A sweet man, it is, indeed," she chortled. "I've never heard such a lie since just before I was married."

Suddenly there was suspicion in the bright eyes that he was mocking her; and a stillness among those who had gathered in the room. Bony felt the menace of sudden violence. It was a risk he had calculated early that morning when he had gathered selected gum leaves, and subsequently practised playing on them again.

With a leaf between his fingers, and the edge of it against his lips, he rendered 'Danny Boy', the reedy notes being low and of a texture which no fiddle could imitate. It did not matter that he failed to play it well. It was this new musical accompaniment to the remembered song which captivated his audience, for he trod the bridge, the only bridge spanning the gulf from the ancient race to the new one ruling Australia: the bridge of music. The vibrating leaf sent forth its last note, and instead of bowing and looking for compliment, the wily Bony stood with head drooping as though he were one with all the persecuted ones.

A fire log hissed. The roast in the oven snoozed. A man said:

"Play it again, Nat," and Grandma Conway said firmly:

"No. Not again just yet," and began to cry.

A woman went to her, and Mike's wife called for assistance in serving the dinner. The others drifted to their places at the table, and for the first time Bony felt the relaxation of reserve towards him.

"Is it hard to play on a leaf?" asked a much freckled girl of perhaps fifteen.

"Not very," replied Bony, smiling.

"Do all the natives in the outback play on gum leaves?" a boy wished to know.

"Not all of the station aborigines do," replied Bony. "The real wild ones can only play on a didgerido, a length of hollow wood. It isn't music as we understand music. They can beat in time with their ceremonial dances, but I'm sure they could never play an Irish tune."

It was as if a river had burst its banks. The previous reticence was swept away by the eager questioning of the child-

34

ren. Rosalie Conway set before Bony a platter of Irish stew as though it were an honour bestowed on him for his musical talent, and even the adults were interested enough to listen to his replies.

"We'll pick some leaves and play on 'em while Uncle Joe grinds on his concertina," declared the boy on Bony's right.

"I like that," objected the bald man. "Grinding on me concertina."

Another boy enthused:

"We'll have a band like they do on television. Instead of fiddles we'll have gum leaves."

"You boys keep quiet and eat your dinner," commanded Mike Conway without raising his voice, and his control over this family was instantly proved. At Bony's end of the table there was silence.

The back-drop of the great pictures, the grandfather clock, the several copper warming pans hanging on the wall, and the small bric-à-brac on mantel and shelves completed a memorable setting for the man seated at the lower end of the great table.

He was thinking this when a bell rang.

It was inside an old-fashioned domestic bell-indicator box, affixed to the wall just inside the passage door. The conversation at the head of the table abruptly ceased. Bald-headed Uncle Joe, left his chair and, crossing to the indicator, flicked up the dropper covering numeral one. Unhurriedly, Mike Conway left his seat and came to Bony, saying:

"Visitors, Nat. Better go to your room and shut down the trap. I'll let you know when they've gone."

Bony nodded. Watched by the others, he sauntered to the back door, noting that several sympathised with him at having to leave during a meal. Rosalie Conway did not look at him. She sat immobile as though examining a fruit beetle among the portion of blackberry pie she had in her spoon.

Having closed the back door behind him, he paused for a moment to accustom his eyes to the dark of early night, and to spend a moment listening for an approaching car or other vehicle. Hearing nothing, he passed between Conway's house and the open-fronted shed building, coming to the edge of the only road through the settlement.

At the entrance to the shed he stopped again, and now observed the headlights of a motor vehicle coming down the zig-zagging track from the white house on the ridge. He could just hear the hum of its engine. There was another sound, a low whirring noise. It came from the house opposite. Against the pale sky where the light of the departed day still lingered, he witnessed the dwarfing of a television mast. The antenna was ultimately telescoped into the roof.

CHAPTER 5

Peace and War

THE UNLIT lamp was on the table in his room. The trap was up and poised on a stick. The way of retreat was clear. Bony waited within the dark interior of the shed. Without effort his ear registered the noise of the oncoming car.

He was convinced that the warning bell was associated with this visit, and also that the visit had been announced to the occupants of the opposite house who had immediately telescoped their television antenna. For the first time since coming to Cork Valley, the curtain was lifted a little on these Cork Valley people.

"No one has ever gone in there and discovered anything of an illegal nature," Superintendent Casement had said.

Who had rung the warning bell, and from where had it been rung? Bony reflected on the journey he had made by truck from the white house on the ridge. He estimated the time taken from the white house to the settlement, minus the period spent on replacing the damaged tyre, and was convinced that unless the warning had been delayed at the white house, it hadn't been given there.

It was as well he was not outside the shed entrance, for the headlights suddenly illuminated the entire settlement, causing him to withdraw farther inside, and enabling him to see three men crossing the roadway diagonally to meet the oncoming vehicle. When it stopped outside the general store, they converged on the car, and Bony saw for a second the figures of Mike Conway and Joe Flanagan before the headlights were snapped off.

There was no talk. The slamming of doors told him that the men had entered the car, and it passed the shed and went on down the roadway with its lights out. Bony waited to hear it stop at the cheese factory. But he heard it pass the factory and fell to pondering on its destination. Beyond the factory there were no houses, nothing but the large piggery. The car went on beyond the piggery.

As immobile as the corner post of the shed, Bony listened to the sound of the car dwindling into the distance. He watched the mast rising from the opposite house against the starry sky. He watched another rising from a house farther along the row. Still without lights, the car pressed on in the same direction, moving slowly, but not stopping. It was obvious that the driver knew the way, every yard of it.

The visitors were not police, and Bony wondered if Mike Conway was aware of their identity before their arrival. It was unlikely because the television masts had been lowered before their arrival, and raised again shortly after they had gone on, when it was known who they were.

The now faint noise of the car abruptly ceased. In the silence he could hear music coming from a house, the gurgling of the small river beyond the settlement, and fancied he could detect among the night sounds that of the far away waterfall.

How long he stood there resting his back against the corner post didn't bother him until he heard the car returning. Its headlights were still not operating when it passed the shed and stopped outside the store. Again the doors were slammed, and then the track was brilliantly lit by the headlights, and within the side glow he counted the three men who had come from the neighbouring house, and the two from the Conway place. When the car drove off, he thought it time for discretion, and slipped down into his cellar where he lit the lamp and pretended to be interested in a paperback autobiography.

He was left undisturbed and the following morning his day began as usual. The settlement was still in shadow. The first milking was almost done, the milked cows waiting in the yard at the rear of the shed and the last batch waiting in a side yard to take their places under the machines. Passing along the roadway he saw a woman shaking a mat outside her front door, two others gossiping and a gaffer pottering in a garden. The scene was normal. A beagle came and wagged his tail, and Bony paused to pat him.

Dogs! He recalled that the previous night scene had been incomplete, for no dogs voiced hostility or welcome to the night visitors. How had they been controlled? Quite a mystery to think about while digging potatoes.

There can be no two opinions about the Australian autumn, when the days are softly warm and the nights are cool and placid; the heat and the dust and hot winds of summer are irritants easily forgotten. This was another perfect autumn day in Cork Valley. At the end of the houses, Bony turned off the road and followed a path into low scrub, which soon gave place to open gums, and beyond them he entered a wide lane between wire fences. The path skirted the river, now merely a stream running over polished granite stones and washing against the larger boulders. Magpies warbled and one dive-bombed him and then gave it up. He crossed the river by a narrow bridge, where the path junctioned with a wider track on which were the marks of motor tyres and horses hooves.

Half a mile on, he had to leave the track and follow another across the grass paddocks to reach his bagged potatoes and digging fork, and place his lunch bag and billy on a large stone fallen from the old dividing wall.

The wall reminded him of a part of Victoria where the stones had been gathered and built to serve as fences. This one appeared to have neither beginning nor end. It came up over a rise to the north, passed him by and ended amid the trees marking the river to the south. Where he was working was its highest point. Here it had weathered best, being four feet high and four feet wide. The stones comprising it had obviously been gathered from the adjacent land, so that old Mrs Kelly had really achieved a dual purpose when she ordered its erection . . . peace and improvement of the land.

He, too, was now at the highest point of the valley floor. The track from the house on the ridge down to the settlement was like a crayon mark. The settlement shone like a white mausoleum on green velvet. The waterfall beyond was molten silver. Beyond the wall the great house occupied by the Kellys stared suspiciously with its many eyes at him.

He could see the children running and playing in the only street of the settlement, on their way to the school building. Two men were working near the cream factory, and two others were driving the cows to pasture. Another was riding a horse in a distant paddock on the Kelly side of the wall. Crows cawed about the yard, which, by the skins drying on racks, must have been the slaughtering place, and a blue wren danced on top of one of his potato bags.

It was a pastoral scene, to engage the enthusiasm of an artist. All about him vistas of peace and beauty. Children going to school; houses where people lived unaware of the joys of television . . . by day. A liqueur at the end of dinner strong enough to choke any damned Englishman. Cars going about without headlights and engaged in mysterious business. This Cork Valley had slumbered for centuries, disturbed now and then by domestic arguments among the aborigines, had swooned beneath the summer sun, and was cosily wrapped about from the winter cold.

Until the Kellys came. They stirred the stuffing out of it. They built the big house, built the wall and cleaned the land of stones. They said it was their land, and it was so. Had Sean Kelly ridden up that track gashing the slopes to find himself a wife? Had he ridden down that track with a wife on the saddle behind him? By which road had his sister Nora gone forth to seek a husband, to return with a man of derring-do, and two priests to make sure of subsequent respectability? Where, just where, had the husbands met with pistols blazing, and left their widows and children to carry on a tradition of violence until an old woman with a last will and testament cried: "Peace or else"? And the wall was built, and peace of a kind came to Cork Valley.

That tough old woman had been born again in the strong-willed old woman even now pointing her telescope at the spud digger. She could pipe the eye on hearing 'Danny Boy' played on a gum leaf, but it was on record that she had used an axe handle for a purpose not intended, when she had laid out a stranger caught stealing her cattle.

"Superficially they're all quiet and peaceful," Superintendent Casement had told Bony. "But, privately, I'm game to bet my rabbit burrow is down there."

A kookaburra came to rest on the bag next to the one where the blue wren had danced. Another came to perch on the edge of the wall. Silently Bony welcomed them, and hoped they would repeat their previous performances. He dug on and on, action methodical and now tireless, and with the appearance of the potatoes, there also appeared large and fat worms. The kookaburras chortled softly at each other, and then one after the other flew to land within a yard of his implement and gobble the worms. Finally they waited within inches of the fork for the worms to be uncovered.

Bony talked to them. Their beady eyes divided attention between him and the earth, and when he paused both looked at him and waited as though plainly asking why the heck he had stopped digging. He was thus engaged when he heard the thudding hooves of an approaching horse. He straightened up when a cheerful voice called:

"Day to you! How's the crop?"

"Good day" responded Bony. The birds flew away, and he strolled to the wall where he had put his coat, and from a pocket produced tobacco and papers. The man on the horse was in his middle twenties, and there was no need to ask his name for he was of the same mould as the red giant who had rushed Bony into the shed. "Another great day, eh?"

"Beaut! Are you the horse thief?"

Inwardly Inspector Bonaparte flinched, but calmly he replied:

"Well . . . yes. Who are you?"

"I'm a Kelly. My name's Brian. What's yours? I did hear but I've forgotten."

Bony who liked frankness in other people, began to like this Brian Kelly. The grey eyes were wide and candid. He had his father's colouring and the promise of his father's physical power in the wide shoulders and the powerful neck. The voice was pleasing. The somewhat weathered riding togs were less so.

"The name is Nathaniel Bonnay. Nat for short. I met your

father, I think, the day I arrived. You live in a nice place."

"Nice enough on fine days, Nat. Leaks a bit when it rains. Nothing wrong with the country though. Except for the fogs. Though I like the fogs, as a matter of fact. They prevent people spying on others, like Grandma Conway's doing right now."

"She is, eh!"

"Have a deck," Brian Kelly waved a hand towards the settlement. "Parks herself at the eye-piece of a glass all day. Don't miss much, the old witch."

Bony could see the sunlight glinting from behind a window adjacent to the general store.

"I'll be told tonight that I don't work fast enough."

The younger man loaded a pipe, watching Bony at the same time with his small shrewd eyes. The wide mouth was generous, but the chin betrayed a quick temper. The flame-red hair needed cutting, and the cloth cap clamped down on it needed replacing. Bony knew that his mother had been dead several years. He knew, too, that Brian Kelly had, like the Conways in their turn, been educated at a Catholic college. That costs money and money was here in this valley. Yet Brian Kelly's clothes were disgracefully worn, and could be his father's cast-offs.

"Are you working for wages?"

"Contract. Seven shillings a bag," replied Bony.

"Oh!" The pipe was lit, and Brian gazed pensively across the paddocks towards the settlement. "Where are they camping you?"

"In the cellar under the shed."

"I've never been down there. Heard about it. Good hideaway, though. I understand they feed well. We eat like dogs."

"Mrs Conway is a wonderful cook," Bony said. "Seems to have plenty of help, too."

"They're civilised; we're still savages." He was sitting on the saddle sidewise, and the horse was placidly standing parallel with the wall. A faint smile touched his mouth.

"Didn't think there was anything in horses these days. Stealing them, I mean," he prompted, and Bony laughed and explained that the horses which had been his downfall were

42

prospective racing stock. Brian wanted to know the details. He wanted to know what the country was like round Tenterfield. He asked if there was much employment in the real outback, and was pressing his questions when his face fell into a dark frown.

"The old man's coming to argue," he stated with conviction, adding with equal conviction. "I'm fed to the back teeth with the old man."

Red Kelly was coming on fast, mounted on a grey mare that was feeling his spurs and crop. He was wearing smart jodhpurs and a tweed jacket, and the breeze was parting his bushy red beard and overgrown red hair. He arrived at speed, cruelly sawing at the animal's bit. Ignoring Bony nonchalantly leaning against the wall, he shouted with unnecessary violence at his son.

"You get to hell out of here. Get on with your work. Go on, get away from here. I'll not stand for you gossiping with every Tom, Dick and Harry, and horse-thieves and scum off the roads. Get going."

Young Kelly sat on his horse without moving. His face was white, and his eyes appeared to reflect the colour of his father's beard. With shattering swiftness the elder man slashed his crop across his son's face, whisking the pipe from his son's mouth.

"I'm the boss of Cork Valley," he yelled. "I say go, you go. You been looking for a thrashing for a long time, my lad, a long, long time."

Brian Kelly partly fell, partly slipped from his horse. He made a crouching run to the grey. Red Kelly lifted his crop to strike again. He was seized by a foot and tossed off his horse.

CHAPTER 6

A Private Fight

THE QUESTION in Bony's mind was: 'Is this a staged brawl for the purpose of involving me and resulting in a trip to hospital, like that policeman?' Such violence between father and son could, however, be genuine, and in either case Bony was presented with a ring-side seat.

Kelly gained his feet, blinked his small, turquoise eyes, and roared his fury. The protagonists were of the same height, but the older man had superior weight, and probably greater strength, despite his age. Bony settled down to enjoy a good match, as any man would do in a stadium. Yells, shouts, grunts and threats, combined with smacks like a storm-ripped sail, and welling gore, aroused in this man of two races instincts which he would normally be ashamed to reveal.

Now he was standing on the wall and yelling encouragement. The evenness of the battlers, their ferocity, the blood smearing their faces and fists drove from Bony's mind what he was and had achieved, and all his maternal ancestors crowded in to take possession.

At one moment the son was standing on his father's chest, and with both hands trying to tear the beard off him. At the next the son was staggering away and the father was on his feet. Then the father had his son in his arms and was straining to crack his ribs. Tearing himself from his father's grip, Brian snatched up a seven-pound rock.

The rock rose and the rock descended on Red Kelly's head. Red Kelly rolled forward on his side, flung his arms about his son's ankles and brought him down. For perhaps a half-minute they were like little playful bears and then the younger man was on his back and the older man's huge hands were about his throat. A vast heaving struggle slowly subsided and there was the horrific flutter of life about to depart.

Nat Bonnay proved to be the hangman's nark. He jumped

from the wall on to Red Kelly and dragged him back by the hair. As this was an unbelievable impertinence, Red Kelly heaved himself upward, threw Bony off his back and prepared to charge. But Bony was on his feet a fraction ahead of him, and the toe of Bony's boot connected with Kelly's chin grounding him like a plane without wings.

As one Kelly struggled to regain air and the other strove to return from a far journey, Bony was jigging on his feet: a delighted David triumphant over two Goliaths. When Red Kelly opened his dazed blue-washed eyes, he encountered eyes of indigo blue, and Brian Kelly lurched to his feet, swayed dizzily, and yelled:

"What are you doing, you black bastard? Keep out of this. It's a private fight."

He rushed Bony, shorter than himself by six inches, and lighter by three to four stone. Bony wasn't there, and before he could swing about, he was being ridden like Sinbad. Bony rode high, and he did things to Brian's neck with steel-like fingers in the manner of his mother's knowledgeable people. Searing pain shot into Brian's brain, unendurable and unending pain. He heard as though beyond the sea of pain the hissed words:

"I can send you mad, you young idiot. Pipe down."

Then he was free of the pain but not of the knifing memory of it. He realised he was kneeling and sobbing. He heard his father shouting that he would murder the black bastard. The shouts turned into screams of rage, and the screams terminated in an earth shaking thud.

On Brian Kelly raising his head and looking about with one effective eye, he saw his father on hands and knees, the hands on one side of an earth-based boulder and the knees on the other, his shrinking stomach athwart the crown of rock. He began to crawl towards his sire, savage hate reborn, but when Red Kelly sprawled forward on his face and groaned, Brian crawled to his horse, clawed his way up and into the saddle, and rode dejectedly towards the big house.

Ten minutes later, Red Kelly lurched to his feet, staggered to the grey mare, hauled himself into the saddle, and rode after his son. He seemed to have forgotten all about the spud digger.

Working through the afternoon, Bony gave part of his attention to the scenery beyond the stone wall, accepting the probability that the Kellys might re-enter the arena accompanied by reinforcements. The blue wren, fed full on the insects uncovered by the digging fork prior to the battle, lazed on the filled bags of potatoes, and the kookaburras returned to levy their tax on the worms.

On entering the Conways' living-room for dinner, it was instantly apparent that the entire clan was waiting for him. The matriarch in her high back chair before the open hearth greeted him with:

"Come here, young feller, and give an account of yourself."

A lace cap instead of a wig. A black dress instead of an ermined gown. But the same penetrating eyes of the judge, the same pseudo-placidity hiding the iron will to extract facts. Bony sensed the tense atmosphere. He felt rather than witnessed the others ranged beside and behind him. It was time for cunning, and for this he was not unprepared.

"Well, go on, Nat. What happened?"

He could have earned millions of dollars on the films instead of his miserable salary as a homicide investigator. In the assumed character of the State-educated but not fully assimilated half-aborigine, he shuffled his feet, looked everywhere save into the expectant faces about him, and into those probing dark eyes. Then, as though forcing himself to speak, he said:

"How did you know about the Kellys? None of you was there."

"I was there. Through my spyglass I was there," sternly countered the old woman.

"Oh!" Again the nervous shuffling of feet. The faint hunching of the shoulders betrayed instinctive shrinking. "Well, it happened like this." Now there was defiance in his voice. "I had to defend myself, see! A young chap who said he was Brian Kelly came along where I was working. He was pleasant enough. Said it looked like the potato crop was heavy, and all

46

that. Then his father came galloping across the paddocks, and told him to get back to work. When he wouldn't go, his father hit him with his riding crop. Hit him across the mouth and knocked the pipe out. So the young chap jumped off his horse and heaved his father off his, and they got stuck into it."

"Yes, yes! I saw all that," shrilled the now ecstatic old woman. "I could see their heads above the wall, and you standing on the wall and dancing with excitement. Then you jumped off the wall and joined in. I saw that, too."

"Well, I thought they were just having a bit of a blue. Old Kelly fell down, and young Kelly stood on his chest with both feet and tried hard to pull the beard off him. Mr Kelly got rid of his son and they charged together and wrestled a bit, and Brian kneed his father, and then took up a rock and tried to brain him. Then they had another wrestle, and this time Mr Kelly got down hard to the job of strangling his son. I had to stop him with a drop kick."

"I didn't see that," complained old Mrs Conway. "Go on."

"Well, I thought that finished the blue," continued Nat Bonnay. "It took some time for Brian to get over the strangling, and his old man to get over my drop kick. Mr Kelly stood up first, and Brian called me a black bastard, which I resent. Anyway, Mr Kelly came for me. He had five yards to travel, and he sort of got up speed. When he got to me he had one foot high in a try to kick me. I got both hands under his foot, and at the same time he began to straighten his leg and so sort of levered himself up on my hands."

"Ha!" The ejaculation was whispered between the old woman's parted lips. "I saw Red Kelly go up twice as high as the wall. I'll swear to it, 'deed I will. And it was you that sent him, Nat?"

Nat Bonnay was now distinctly nervous. He looked up from the floor. He glanced into those burning dark eyes and hastily looked at Mike Conway standing beside him, and then at the flaming logs.

"Did you send Red Kelly up twice as high as the wall? That great red bull of an Irishman? Did you?" persisted Mrs Conway.

"Well, I had to do something to stop 'em," replied Nat, now a clear whine in his voice. "Mr Kelly was strangling his son, all right. Brian's face was purple and his tongue was poking out. I didn't want any killing, and the police coming down here and dragging me into it. I got troubles enough. It's all right for you squatters. You got the police on your side. You always have had 'em on your side."

Nat paused for breath, and was conscious of the silence in the room. He went on, half fearful, half rebellious.

"There was Mr Kelly rushing me, and Brian was coming out of the fit and trying to join in. As I said, Mr Kelly stepped into my hands and sprang off them. I had to fix him because he was getting vicious, and so as he heaved up, I twisted my hands so he'd come down with his stomach landing fair and square on a handy half buried rock. It made him terrible sick, but I'm not pulling my forelock and sayin' I'm sorry."

In that large and homely room there was silence, prolonged, imprisoned. The grandfather clock for which Inspector Bonaparte would have paid five hundred pounds, had he had five hundred pounds, ticked its majestic tread through the Hall of Silence until insulted by an unleashed storm of laughter. Old Mrs Conway gasped and shrieked. She beat the arms of her chair with her fragile blue-veined hands. Mike Conway stooped and flailed his hands against his thighs. His wife clung helplessly to another woman as helpless as herself. Joe Flanagan rocked on his bandy legs to one of which clung a toddler undecided whether to be frightened or happy. Only the girl, Rosalie Conway was coldly disapproving. She stood stiffly, hands at her sides, her face solemn, her eyes closed.

Mike Conway managed to straighten himself and point at Nat, and yell:

"He just twisted his hands under Red's foot so that he came down with his guts across a rock. Him . . . our Nat . . . who weighs eleven stone heaves high old Red and drops his seventeen stone square on a rock. Boy oh boy! If only I could have seen it."

"I did, I tell you," gasped the old woman. "I saw it all through me spyglass. I saw him going up and I watched him coming down. The dratted wall stopped me seeing him spread his stomach on the rock, though." She broke into a gale of laughter, gurgled and gasped and shrieked, and managed to utter words making the sense of: "Made Red terrible sick! My! My! Stop me someone . . . stop me."

The alarmed women gathered about old Mrs Conway and the men were shushed. With difficulty they quieted the matriarch, and eventually dinner was placed on the table.

Nat Bonnay was promoted to a seat beside the old lady whose oaken heart was pacified by a nip of 'wine'. Dinner proceeded with the usual decorum, which hinted of aristocratic ancestors back in Old Ireland. The incident of the gumleaf playing which appeared to have cracked the social ice was now supported by the encounter with the Kellys which melted the ice entirely.

They baffled him, these Conways. Bony had met every kind of Irishman in the outback, men of every degree. Those Irishmen, however, he had known individually. He had seen them against a background of other nationalities. Now he was seeing a family, a clan, against its own background of an isolated valley, haunted by five or six past generations, and he wondered how much the people about this massive table were influenced by their isolation, and how much by their forbears who came from Ireland to fight and claw a foothold in this new, mysterious and hostile land.

He recalled his assignment to mind; to investigate the suspected murder of an excise officer.

Dinner ended and the women and children withdrew, save old Mrs Conway. Mike served the usual cup of liquor, and when they were smoking, he said to Nat:

"No doubt you're thinkin' we're a funny crowd, Nat. We are. We keep to ourselves. All for one and one for all, as the saying goes. Pity you interfered between the Kellys. Mind you, I'd have given a fiver to have seen you in action, but if I had been there I would have joined them against you."

"Damn it, Mike," exploded Nat Bonnay. "I had to separate 'em, as I told you."

"No, you didn't have to, Nat. It was a family fight. It'll work

49

out peaceful in the end. We've had these brawls for years, a hundred and fifty years, from what we've been told. You just go along quietly and keep to your spud digging."

"I'll do that," Nat Bonnay promised. "In fact, I'll pack up and leave the valley if you like."

"No good," argued Conway. "Too late, anyway. Because you are working for the Conways, up to a point you're a Conway. You barge into a fight between the Kellys and a Conway barges in. You took part in a private Kelly fight, and you had no business to. That might start a feud that could go on for years. It's what we don't want, a feud."

"I get it, Mike," Nat said, earnestly.

"Wise man, Nat," old Mrs Conway approved. "In course of time us Cork Valley Irish got a bit of sense and learned that if we don't live peaceful together we'll be scattered peaceful all over Australia." She looked at him long and steadily, and an iron will maintained captive the humorous quirk in her eyes and about her mouth. "You made yourself a Conway man, Nat. You're a Conway, and what's done to you is done to the Conways."

CHAPTER 7

The Dinkum Irish

THREE DAYS passed without sight of the Kellys, and when the sun popped up above the mountain rim on the morning of the fourth day, the potato digger was removing his coat preparatory to beginning work.

Working at contract rates is ever a spur. Bony filled four bags with potatoes on his first day. That was overworking un-used muscles and the day after, the tally wasn't quite four. The next day he filled five, and thence progressed to average ten.

This morning Bony set to work with a will, determined to raise his tally to eleven before the sun popped down. It was another beautiful day and the light clouds scudded across the sky to find the sea. The kookaburras came, and it did seem that, like the platypus, each could consume its own weight in worms every hour. By lunch time, Bony had added six filled bags to the stack.

The wind dictated the making of the fire hard against the stone wall, and the lunch tea having been made, Bony sat with his back to the wall and ate thick slices of ham with thick slices of bread covered generously with butter. He could see his bag stack, could count again the six filled this day, and feel satisfaction from his effort, and still further cause for satis-faction when multiplying six bags by seven shillings per bag, and making two pounds and two shilling for the morning.

Life was good. Inspector Bonaparte was feeling fine. His body was fit, and his mind was clear. He could taste the ham. He could smell the scent of the gum trees. His lungs appre-ciated the clean air. His daily cigarette consumption was down fifty per cent. There was old Mrs Conway watching him through her spyglass, for the sun was reflected by its lens behind the window, and she had said: "Now you're a Conway. What's done to you, Nat, is done to the Conways." It was good to be a Conway. To the devil with Superintendent Casement and his bodies.

The cows were lying down and chewing their cud. The blue wren was almost asleep on the bags and the kookaburras were so heavy in the crop they could do nought but stare. Only old Mrs Conway was fidgeting this late April day. Even the bees, working late and sluggishly, told of peace in Cork Valley. Even the voice above Bony was sweetly solicitous.

"Where will you be havin' it, Nat?"

The wind took the words and carried them past the indifferent kookaburras. Bony, looking upward, saw the boulder suspended over his head, the arms supporting it, the flaming red hair and beard of Red Kelly. How fast does a hundredweight of granite fall eight feet? Eight feet because it was held high by Red Kelly who was standing on the wall. Too fast to permit a side roll to escape it, too fast to make any other move. It was a time for instinct to rule, not reason. Red Kelly's eyes were tawny with lust, and a devilish grin spread his whiskers. In his eyes was the knowledge that he couldn't continue to poise the boulder for longer than another two seconds. Bony said:

"Come on down. I want to talk."

The boulder was tilted to the right. It thudded upon the earth. Red Kelly breathed deeply and flexed his arms. Bony wiped his forehead with his shirt sleeve, and the wind came coldly to complete the drying of perspiration. One thing only was less certain than that death had been in Kelly's eyes was that old Mrs Conway had seen him on the wall and had tried to warn Nat Bonnay. There was now no movement of her glass. The giant sprang from the wall, planted his feet either side of his boulder, sat on it, placed his huge fists on his knees and shouted:

"That's what could happen to you any time. Squashed like a fly. If you had tried to move you'd have got it. *You* want to talk, do you? Well, talk."

"I shall," assented Bony, emphasising the pronoun, and again stressed the pronoun when adding: "You will listen. You Irish are loaded with imagination. It's why the Irish have produced so many great poets and writers. It's why most of you

Irish think you can't be wrong, ever. You have a one-sided mind. Nice looking bird you'd have been with the beard pulled off your face, a rope around your neck and a trap under your feet for strangling your own son. You owe me something."

" 'Tis a lie," yelled Red Kelly.

"Shuppergob! You've said it: I talk."

The exploded words opened Kelly's mouth to yell again, and words exploded again to close it.

"I said: *shut up*."

The light blue eyes blazed with hot fury, and Bony was relieved, for had they blazed with cold fury the situation would have been distinctly dangerous. His own blue eyes were glacial and as the trainer holds the mind of a lion, so now did he hold Red Kelly.

"If I hadn't climbed up behind you and rasped your nose with my arm, you'd have had your son buried and you would have been holing up in your house waiting the police to take you." Bony went on, each word like the crackle of small arms heard at distance. "You may like arguing with the police over a murder. I don't like arguing with 'em over a horse or two. I don't want 'em on any condition. I'm not a big capitalist squatter like you. I'm only a working man. I don't own miles of land. I own only my liberty. And if ever I see you choking anyone else I'll drop kick you so hard you'll sleep for a week. You'd have murdered your son, but you won't admit it to yourself even now. You're not big enough to thank a feller for keeping your neck unstretched. It's the way you dinkum Irish have of kidding yourselves you're the salt of the earth."

The glare in the big man's eyes made lamps of them. The great thighs tightened in the thick gaberdine trousers as the legs tensed to spring. The wide mouth was like a split gibber half buried in red sand. Then fury passed from Red Kelly, and he said, normally:

"Did you say dinkum . . . dinkum Irish?"

"I did."

"Meaning?"

"That you're all guts and no guile."

"Come again."

"That you're so anxious to knock a man that you never pause to think he might have done you a good turn. Which I did."

"And a good turn for yourself at the same time, eh?" queried the still undeflated Kelly.

"In this particular instance it so happens that I don't want the police on my back. Besides . . ."

"Besides what?"

"Besides, I must have a cup or two of Irish blood in me. I can get worked up. The trouble is I can't separate a private fight from a public one. If my mother had been real Irish, I'd know it every time."

Red Kelly was still breathing heavily, but he was tending to deflate and when he produced a clasp knife big enough to slaughter a bullock, Bony was no longer perturbed. A pipe and tobacco appeared, and chips were flaked from the plug while the pipe dangled amid the red whiskers.

"If you was Irish," Kelly managed to say, "you could battle with all the Conways at the same time. Where did you learn that drop kick?"

"A professional wrestler showed me."

"Show me, Nat?"

"No. Every time you used it you would commit murder without intention. You'd kick a man's head clean off his shoulders. No, I wouldn't show you."

"I might be askin' you nice and kindly like."

Menace was again in the voice. The pipe still dangled. The knife stuck up in one fist like a bayonet. Bony explained easily.

"You and I might get into another brawl, when I'd want something to play with. I lifted a policeman off his feet one time. He was very sick. I could have hanged for it."

"A policeman!" shouted Kelly. "Pity you never murdered the bastid."

"You won't say that when I tell you he's Irish."

"Irish was he! A bastid Irishman, that's what he was. The police force's full of 'em. So's the dirty government. They's deserted the Irish, true and sweet." The pipe fell unheeded to the ground, and Red Kelly crammed into his mouth the chips

54

he had sliced from the plug. "They're all bastid Irish, Nat. Mr Rory O'Connell, the premier. Mr Patrick Felix, the Chief Commissioner of Police. Mr Bastid Irish and Mr Bastid that. All in top jobs a-taxin' decent folk. Makin' us pay tax to run a truck, to own a wireless or a television. Piling taxes on a man's tobacco and his whisky. For why? You tell me, Nat. Then I'll tell you. So's they can get free trips round the world, and take their wives and lackey's with 'em. And real Irishmen, real dinkum Irishmen a-slavin' on the land and down in the mines. The dirty Irish rats a-cringin' and a-crawling to the English. A-bobbin' here and a-bobbin' there, and hopin' like hell to be made lords and dukes."

The granite boulder, on which Kelly was sitting like a cat on a hot cannonball, could perhaps have had less impact on Bony than did this tirade, so unexpected was it and so revealing. In odd corners of Australia he had encountered this bitter attitude towards Irishmen in authority, but always in the poorer classes, never in the squatter class to which Red Kelly obviously belonged. He prodded, knowing it to be unwise yet needing to see more clearly.

"All right, the policeman was a bastard. What about Ned Kelly?"[1]

Red Kelly was shocked. His small eyes became smaller still. A scowl bunched the whiskers about his large mouth. He was disarmed by the earnest expression on the face of Nat Bonnay, the eager student. With forced calm, he said:

"Ned Kelly, sir, was a gintleman. He was what you just said: a dinkum Irishman, the descendant of a line of dinkum Irish men and women. Why, it was the bastid Irish what hanged him. If it hadn't been for those renegades, Ned Kelly and his men would have taken all Victoria from the English. Yes, then all of New South Wales. Ned Kelly was true dinkum Irish. God rest his soul. Didn't you go to school?"

"I read a book about him," admitted Nat.

"It wasn't the right book. Them kind's full of lies."

Red Kelly looked sad and sore of heart. He said sincerely:

[1] Ned Kelly a notorious outlaw, was convicted of murder and hanged in Melbourne on November 11, 1880. He has since become Australia's premier national hero.

" 'Tis a pity your mother wasn't Irish. She'd have learned you the truth. You got a bit of Irish in you, Nat, just a drop or two, as I saw when I had that rock over you." He stood and widened his massive shoulders. "All right, me lad. We call it a draw, you and me. You better get back to your spud digging. What's your day tally now?"

"Ten bags yesterday. Six bags this morning."

"Ten!" shouted Red Kelly. "Ye'll starve to death at that rate. Ye haven't the way of it. I'll show you."

Like a tank, he strode purposefully to the digging fork and snatching it from the ground he waved it like a sword. Bony had worked methodically. He had faced the potato row. He had placed the points of the fork in the ground, driven the tines deep with the pressure of a foot, levered the fork backward and so raised the earth containing the tubers and brought them to the surface. Red Kelly bestrode the potato row. He crouched over it like a crab. With both hands he swung the fork in an arc down from the level of his left shoulder. The impetus drove the tool deep into the ground, and the movement continued in its arc and scooped earth and tubers up and free. All in one continuous movement. As the fork was swung back to the original position, the great feet took Red onward nine inches and the curving stroke was repeated again and again until he was at the far end of the row. There had been not one unnecessary action.

There are tricks and knacks in every trade, and Bony learned many in the trade of digging potatoes, especially those used by men weighing seventeen stone and having the strength of two Bonys. It had taken him forty minutes to fill a bag. He estimated it took Kelly a bare seven minutes. He had to drag the filled bag to the stack; Red Kelly carried his bag as he had held the boulder, like a minister holding a baby at a christening.

"That'll make up the time wasted gossiping. Nat," he shouted. He gazed about the scene and sought sight of the sunlight reflected by Mrs Conway's telescope. "Ha! I'd better be off. I'm in a furrin' country. Good day to you, Nat, me lad. I'll be wantin' you to work for me some time. And don't you ever forget that Ned Kelly was a gintleman, and dinkum Irish at that. You spoke a true word, Nat. Dinkum Irish, it is."

Waving a fist almost gallantly, Red Kelly retrieved his pipe and leaped to the summit of the wall. He waved again and jumped down from it to his own land, and as Bony watched him striding towards his ancestral home, he wondered if he had really discovered the secret of these people of Cork Valley.

CHAPTER 8

The Day Old Frosty Came

BONY TRIED Red Kelly's method of digging potatoes but quickly returned to his own pedestrian way of working with a fork. His business was, indeed, concerned with homicide. He worked methodically, his mind occupied by cabbages and kings rather than spuds. An hour after the departure of Red Kelly he was momentarily startled by a gunshot which came from the direction of the meandering river and was too booming to be anything else but the discharge of a twelve-bore shot-gun. Half an hour after that he was startled by hearing the voice of Joseph Flanagan.

"Day to you!"

The shot-gun under Joe's left arm, and the rabbit dangling from his right hand were proof of the way he was spending the afternoon. Here was another character who had defeated Time. He wore cord trousers tucked into rubber boots. About his rangy torso hung a gamekeeper's coat with a pocket capacity for a dozen rabbits and half a dozen pheasants. On his head was a felt hat with the brim cut away except at the front where it formed a kind of sun visor.

Bony called a goodday, and Joe leaned the gun against the potato stack, went to where Bony was working, squatted on his heels and loaded a briar pipe. With the skirt of the coat resting on the earth about him, he looked not unlike a sick emu.

"Nice day, Nat. How's the spuds coming along?" he asked, the leathery face at odds with the gentle accentless voice.

"Pretty good, Joe."

"Heard you had some help a while back."

"That's so," agreed Bony. "Red Kelly came over for a yarn and he showed me how to lift spuds. Mrs Conway tell you about it?"

"Yes. Got quite worried about you. Asked me to work up a hare or two over this way. Seen any about?"

"Two between here and the river yesterday morning. You having the day off?"

"I have lots of days off, Nat, lots of days. Nothing much goes wrong with my installations. Good life, you know. Not much work and plenty of grub, with a nip or two tossed in to keep the flies away. What about a nip now?"

Joe removed from his coat a quart bottle. Bony shook his head; Joe unscrewed the plastic cap, and vapour appeared in the sunlight. He winked, tilted the bottle to his mouth and swallowed twice without winking.

"Not as mellow as Mike's dinner wine," he remarked, replacing the bottle. "Comes from over the hills and far away. Nat. They haven't the knack of it. One of these dark nights they'll blow themselves up. Still, there must be a good trade for it. With the taxes off, it comes reasonable in price. Red Kelly's in a bad temper, they say."

There was the invitation, and Bony knew it would be unwise to evade it. He described the boulder dropping incident, and how he had managed to get himself "out from under".

"The old lady saw it all," contributed Joe. "Tried to warn you with her glass that Red was creeping up on you. If you see her glass blinking and going on, accept them flashes as a warning, and go to ground. You liking it around here?"

"Could do when I get to understand the people."

Joe drew at the pipe, flopped to relieve the pressure of his heels under his posterior, and for a few moments watched the tubers appearing above Bony's fork before saying:

"Depends a lot on yourself, Nat. I been here eleven years. Took me a year to understand 'em. Very clannish even for us Irish. Don't take to strangers too easily, but warm enough when they do. Anyway, you've got on fast with the Conways, especially with the old lady. You could dig in with them for the rest of your life if you wanted to."

"I don't want to dig spuds for the rest of my life, Joe."

"Don't have to. Plenty of easier ways of getting on in Cork Valley. Anyway, a feller ought to push his roots down somewhere." Joe squinted his eyes. "Ah, there's Old Frosty. As I was saying. Nat, the Conways have sort of taken to you, but the main thing is to be satisfied with simple things. I stay on here for a full year, and at the end of it I've got enough money to take a trip. Went to Europe last year. Went to the States the year before. I'm planning to trip over to South America next year." Joe stood. "Well, I'd better put up a hare if there's one to be got. Mate Conway can jug a hare better than anyone I know."

"Then you get that hare," Bony urged. "Who's Old Frosty?"

"Old Frosty? Why, that cloud over to the south. Sure sign of coming frosts and fogs. The fogs hang around for days. So long, Nat. See you at dinner."

Joe Flanagan gathered his gun, stuffed the rabbit into a pocket and ambled across the green fields. Old Frosty was long and narrow and wafer-like, and Bony was reminded of Casement saying: "What goes on down in those valleys when the fog is thick and continuous is anybody's business."

Old Frosty came, moving grandly from the south, and the wild west wind died away. Joe Flanagan fired both barrels of his gun, but Bony couldn't see him as he was in a fold of the ground. Bony knew that he hadn't just chanced to come this way, that Mrs Conway had sent him to ease her curiosity, and he wondered if Mike Conway had supplemented the errand by having Joe probe a little, and to offer him inducement to become a man of Cork Valley. Certainly no man on wages, or even contract, could afford to travel across the world every year, and Joe Flanagan was only a tradesman electrician. Was he a ferret who had learned to live with foxes?

Joe Flanagan's way of life had much to commend it. A man isn't mentally defective to work on an outback station for twelve months. With the money saved he lives like a millionaire for a fortnight or three weeks in a city. However, he would need to be richer than a fortnight-millionaire to travel round the world every year. A Red Kelly might make enough digging potatoes on contract to do it, but not a Nat Bonnay, and not a Joe Flanagan, from superficial observation.

Joe's conversation had certainly hinted at an invitation to become closer to these people of Cork Valley, and this had followed the veiled acceptance of Nat Bonnay as one of the

Conways, and, therefore, with the people of Cork Valley in general. The purpose of the approach was far from clear, and Bony was sure that, if he proceeded along the line he had adopted, it would eventually be made clear. It was certain that he was accepted in this valley because he was a horse-thief, because he was wanted by the police and was at war with them and because all these reasons supported his assumed character plus the accident of his birth.

The whys were many. Why had he been offered the con-tract to lift potatoes when there were at the settlement, as at the Kelly's farm, men who appeared merely to be pottering around doing light work? In view of the richness of the land, the number of cows being milked, the obvious prosperity of the people, why did they refuse to pay television licences, and go to the trouble and expense of constructing telescoping antennas? Why, when the Education Department offered to provide a school bus to convey the children to the school at Bowral, had the service been obstructed, until the Department. had finally agreed to the school at the settlement, and the teacher to be a Conway. And why had the settlement people declined a Catholic Church school in lieu of the state school? There was the answer to these whys somewhere, and in these answers might well lie the solution of a murder he had been assigned to investigate.

Bony was still teasing these matters when he left his work for 'home' and dinner. He swung down the slope, over the paddocks and so to the wider track in the lane skirting the river. He had not prospected this lane from end to end but guessed that it gave access to Red Kelly's farm from the settle-ment and thus from the road into the valley. The surface was of fine chocolate dust and here he saw his own tracks and those of Joe Flanagan, overlaying horse tracks and the tracks of a cow and her calf.

He heard the calf before he saw it, and also the low voice of the mother. He came on the calf standing on the stony bed of the river, now but a stream, with the cow on the bank. The calf had attempted to cross, slipped, and had a foot caught between two boulders. Just beyond it was the bridge, and beyond the bridge the thick scrub extending to the settlement road.

Bony sat on the edge of the low bridge and removed his boots and socks. Gingerly he walked to the calf, and after slight effort freed its foot and managed to help it to the bank. It was uninjured, and gave no evidence of having been trapped for more than an hour or two, certainly not prior to the passing of Joe Flanagan.

Sitting again on the edge of the bridge, he washed his muddy feet in the slow moving stream and put on his socks. Then he saw a bright object settled among the stones under the surface. The surface was rippled and the object looked not unlike a stiletto; he removed his socks again, and retrieved it and so discovered a metal screwdriver. It was no larger than the tool found in the kit of a woman's sewing machine.

Peculiar place to find a screwdriver from a sewing machine kit.

Having put on socks and boots, Bony returned to the cow and her calf. He pretended to assure himself that the calf was undamaged, and, on again approaching the bridge, his eyes missed nothing of the tracks coming from and to it. He neither paused nor deviated, there being ample cover for a possible watcher, but he did note without difficulty that Joe Flanagan had stopped there. Instead of sitting on the edge of the bridge, he had sat on the soft low bank of the river.

On his way through the scrub, Bony wondered why Joe had sat on the bank. He had shot a rabbit at some point, but he would not have had to step across the stream to pick it up because there was the bridge. It hadn't been the misadventure of the calf, otherwise he would have freed it as easily as Bony had done. Had he been looking for the screwdriver which could well be his? It was the only plausible solution of a little mystery which was merely of passing interest.

Flanagan was already in the dining-room when Bony entered, and he had to give a report on the Red Kelly visit.

"I watched him creeping up on you," Grandma said severely. "I signalled all I knew how. In future, Nat, you keep one eye on this window and if you see my glass signalling back the sunlight, you look for trouble. The big, hulking, red blackguard could have murdered you."

"I spoke soft words to him, Mrs Conway," Bony said, smiling slightly, and the old woman regarded him warmly, saying:

"Indeed you should have been an Irishman, Nat. You've all the blarney in Cork Valley."

He was again sitting at the lower end of the great table with Flanagan on his right and Rosalie Conway on his left. To his surprise and delight they were all served with oysters in the shell, and subsequently with schnapper cutlets garnished with a white sauce which determined him to lay on the blarney with Mate Conway just to coax the recipe from her for his own Marie at home in Queensland.

The women and children having left table, Mike Conway served the white 'wine' in china cups. Flanagan spoke of seeing Old Frosty, and the other men nodded.

"The fogs here are really something," Mike Conway told Bony. "D'you have fogs at Tenterfield?"

"Ground mist in the mornings. It would seem they're pretty thick here though."

"What about going to work and coming home, Nat? Think you could find your way?"

"The fog couldn't be so thick that I couldn't see the ground," Bony claimed. "Follow my own tracks across the paddocks."

"Yes, of course." Conway's dark expressionless eyes came down the length of the table as a graphite pencil mark on white cloth. Flanagan was concentrating on loading his pipe. Mrs Conway was gazing disappointedly into her empty cup. She said:

"Nat could see his way in the dark over the paddocks, up the cliffs, over the peaks and all the way back. I've read about the aborigines. Nat is one of them. He told us so."

"All right, Grandma, all right," Mike said impatiently. "I was only testing Nat so that we need not have to go out looking for him if the fog comes down when he's spud digging."

"Don't worry about me," Bony told them.

Grandma Conway looked from her cup to him. She said: "That's my boy. I'm backing you, Nat."

CHAPTER 9

One of the Conways

THE DAYS following the appearance of Old Frosty indicated that he was a false prophet. They continued as before, sunlit and softly warm; the evenings painting the valley in pastel colours, and the nights cool and quiet. Day by day, the man who had inherited a patience unknown to any race other than the Australian aborigines, worked at his potato lifting and waited in the sure belief that the Mountain did come to Mahomet.

The day after Old Frosty drifted benignly across the sky, two of the Conways came with a truck and removed Bony's stacked bags of potatoes to the piggery which, as previously stated, was farthest from the settlement, beyond the butter and cheese factory. They did not unload during the daylight hours, and the next morning the empty truck was standing outside one of the houses. Then the great heap of pie melons in the shed above Bony's cellar room disappeared while he was at work.

The children were given their end-of-term holidays, and nearly all of them now brought in the cows and pastured them after the milking, and the elder children worked about the factory buildings. Three men, including Joe Flanagan who ate with the Conways, did not appear at dinner on the third night, and on the fifth night, following Old Frosty's appearance, Mate Conway served her jugged hare garnished with blackcurrent jelly. Bony decided that this was the life for him.

On May 10 frost did indeed touch the higher paddocks, and as Bony walked to the potato field, his breath was misty and his face and hands tingled. But of fog there was no sign. The sun dispelled the frost and gave warmth very early and the wind came fitfully from the west and brought with it the scent of burning wheat stubble from the far distant farms where preparations were being made for fallowing.

Here in Cork Valley, there was a change. Where four horses belonging to Red Kelly had grazed, there were now eleven. Although the paddock where they cropped was not less than half a mile away, Bony could recognise Red Kelly's grey mare and the roan gelding usually ridden by Brian Kelly, as well as two other animals he had previously seen on the Kelly side of the wall. He had never seen the remaining seven horses before.

Not only would it require good eyesight to pick out the seven strange horses, but it would need, further, a good eye for a horse. Those four Bony had seen previously were big boned, grass fed and in excellent condition, in spite of the hard work. The seven strangers were all much smaller, and lean and hard.

The obvious explanation was that they had been brought in from an outlying area where the ground feed at the end of summer had given out, but Bony's curiosity was aroused by the uniformity of their physical appearance and the fact that they were a different breed from those already on Kelly's property. Another point about them teased Bony but he failed to determine what it was, the distance defying him.

Later in the morning, Brian Kelly appeared on foot, and the horses stood with raised heads watching his approach. He carried a bridle, and he walked straight to the horse he had ridden the day of the brawl, slipped the bridle about its head, and mounted it bareback. Then he rounded up the mob and drove them from the paddock towards the house, where they could no longer be seen.

Accepting the probability that he was customarily under Grandma Conway's surveillance, Bony was careful not to betray any interest, and he continued his work as though engrossed by the urge to increase his daily tally of spuds.

There was another unusual intrusion into Cork Valley in the mid-afternoon. Old Mrs Conway began to signal. Bony straightened, casually looked about, and saw two men approaching from the west. They were less than a quarter-mile from the wall, and both bore the heavy loads of bush-walkers. Both wore the tough clothes and boots associated with these people who delight in tramping over mountainous country. And mounted on his grey mare, Red Kelly was riding furiously to cut them off.

Bony's impulse was to snatch his coat and lunch bag from the wall and walk away from them; to keep his back to them, and prevent them from seeing his face and recognising his racial ancestry. This would be strictly in keeping with the character of a police-hunted ex-horse-thief, but when he estimated that Red Kelly would halt the bushwalkers before they came too close to be able to identify him, he bent lower over his work and watched the meeting with side-wise glances.

"And where d'you think ye be tramping to?" shouted Red Kelly before reining back his horse. "This is private land, and I'll have you know it. I won't be having you disturbing my stock. Where d'you think you're going?"

Bony couldn't catch the replies, and Red Kelly maintained his indignantly shouted protests, although having reached the trespassers, shouting was quite unnecessary.

"To the coast and Wollongong, eh! Well, this is no road to the coast and Wollongong. How did you get here? What's that! Came down the cliffs with your ropes. More fools you. I've a good mind to have the law on you. We have been losing cattle and how are we to know you're not spying out the land to steal more? I don't want your names. I want you off my property. You come down to the house. There's a truck leaving for town in half an hour. You can go on your way in that."

The wind had fallen, but even had there been a strong gale Red Kelly's voice would have reached Bony. The halted bushwalkers eased their loads, and began the divergent walk down the slope to the house, with Kelly riding behind them as though he were driving two prisoners back to the stockade. He ranted at them continuously until even his mighty voice no longer reached the amused potato digger.

Now what! Were those men sent by Superintendent Casement? Casement had said:

"There must be a plan whereby we can keep in touch. We don't want to find you dead on a road and looking as though you'd been run down by a truck. You have consented to go down to Cork Valley, and we must take reasonable precautions for your safety. We'd better send a dairy inspector, or some such, about once a week, and you could make yourself seen by him. If he doesn't see you . . ."

"It would ruin the set up," Bony had argued. "Not only that. If the position is as you suspect, then the appearance of any stranger, in no matter what guise, would be definitely dangerous. Don't be concerned about me. I'll come up when I am ready, and I'll be ready when I have finalised my assignment, or when I am convinced that Cork Valley isn't where your rabbit burrow is. So, Super, no supervision, no interference."

Casement had grumbled, had been unconvinced, had reluctantly agreed to make no move on being assured that when he, Bony, decided to leave Cork Valley nothing or no one would hinder him.

The odds were against the bushwalkers being Casement's spies. They were within their rights to walk over the mountains, to scale cliffs with their ropes and risk their necks, to camp out in the lee of a rock or beside a stream. It was arguable that they had the right to cross private property and Red Kelly most certainly argued they had not, all the way down the slope to his house.

Later, dust rose from the lane and soon thereafter Bony watched the truck speeding up the track to the top of the rim where was the white house and the boundary fence.

Working on, he planned his 'front' to the Conways in respect to the trespassers, and then he heard a sound which, when he concentrated, he thought must have been made by a blacksmith's hammer clanging on an anvil adjacent to Red Kelly's house. It could mean that the horses had been taken from the paddock to be reshod.

Unless there is work for them, horses are not shod.

The dust from the truck clung to the mountain slopes, and was more evidence that the erratic wind was dropping. Minutes after the vehicle had disappeared over the rim, three horsemen rode from the vicinity of Kelly's house and proceeded in a westerly direction. Bony watched them cautiously. He was almost sure that one was Brian Kelly, and that another was Steve Conway, and that the animals they rode were not any of the seven strangers.

As the sun neared the high western horizon the truck returned and the wind died away to an early evening calm. Bony could now distinctly hear the clanging of the blacksmith's hammer. At five o'clock the sun disappeared, and the blacksmith stopped working. A few minutes later the horses were returned to the paddock, the seven strangers and Red Kelly's grey. At a quarter past five Bony parked his fork, donned his coat, collected his lunch bag and billy can and set off down the slope to the river and settlement. The three horsemen had not yet returned.

Immediately on meeting the Conways in their dining room, Bony asked sharply:

"Who were those two hoboes?"

Grandma Conway continued to gaze at the open fire, and Mike Conway replied:

"A couple of bushwalkers, so they said."

"Oh! How d'you know? Did they prove themselves?"

"They said they were bushwalkers, Nat. They looked the kind. They carried the bushwalkers' kit, including ropes to scale rocks. What's riling you?"

"What's riling me!" echoed Bony, voice raised. "Look! They were making for me, and I wasn't wearing my hat. They could have seen me as not being a hundred per cent white. They would have done if Kelly hadn't stopped them when he did. There's no knowing that they didn't farther back, with binoculars. Were they searched for binoculars? Were they carryin' 'em in cases slung from their necks? Those sort generally do."

"Pipe down, Nat," urged Mike Conway. "Everything's all right. They didn't carry glasses, and Red Kelly thinks they weren't close enough to you to register anything. If you are thinking they are police agents, forget it."

"I'm not thinking that," Bony said. "I am thinking those fellers could tell some of their pals about crossing the valley and being balled up by Red Kelly and seeing me working at the spuds, and that could get to the police."

"Forget it." The aura of strain which had met Bony on entering the room had faded, and he became confident that his tactics had succeeded in allaying suspicion that the bush-walkers were police agents checking on a police agent. He said:

"It's too open up there digging spuds. I don't like it."

Grandma Conway spoke for the first time.

"Nat, me boy, don't be worrying so. It turned out all right for you. Don't be blamin' of us, now. I saw those fellers, and I signalled with me glass long before you looked this way."

Bony permitted himself to be mollified, and he turned a half-smile upon the old woman.

"I'm blaming myself really, Grandma," he began and stopped. "Oh, I'm sorry, Mrs Conway. That was a slip of the tongue. I should have kept looking more often this way. I'll remember to now, for sure."

"You be wiser in future, Nat," she said, and thoughtfully added: "And you can call me Grandma if you like. Everyone does who's a Conway."

Bony beamed. "Then I'll be a-serenading of you, Grandma."

The leaf was between his fingers. The leaf was against his lips, and the preparations for serving dinner were hushed. They heard nothing until Kathleen Mavourneen came across the world from Ireland to be with them, the effect to be credited to the instrument rather than the player.

Due to the insistence of every housewife that when dinner is cooked it must be served, the resulting silence was broken by Mate Conway calling them to the table. Grandma Conway's eyes were bright as she was wheeled from her place before the fire, and Mike was smiling as he rarely did.

Steve Conway appeared late that evening, apologising to Mate Conway, nodding to Grandma and her grandson, and then at Bony when seated, and in the usual manner the meal came to its conclusion. This evening, as he was about to leave, Mike called him to join him and his grandmother who was again seated before the fire. He was invited to sit between them, and the chore of washing utensils and clearing the table went on behind them.

"How do you like being here with us, Nat?" Conway asked.

"I'm finding it suits me," answered Bony. "How do I fit?"

"Pretty good," Conway said, staring at the flames. "How would you like to stay on, say for a year, even always?"

"It wouldn't be hard, Mike. You've all been very decent to me. You mean stay on working for you?"

"Yes. You see, there's not too many men working about the place. Valley's always a little short of labour and that's because we like to keep the place to the Conways and the Kellys. It has always belonged to us, and we don't take to strangers."

"But you took to me that day you gave me a lift," queried Bony.

Mike Conway chuckled before saying:

"Explanation's simple, Nat. I wanted my spuds lifted. You were in a spot of trouble and the Irish have a soft spot for the under dog. In that respect you and us Irish are on equal ground. That's so, Grandma?"

"Yes, 'tis so," agreed the ancient. "You're welcome to stay on with us Conways as a Conway, Nat. You haven't a home, have you?" Bony shook his head.

"You have a wife, though?"

"She cleared off with another man when I was in gaol."

"So you said, Nat."

"And there's other work beside digging spuds all day," Mike contributed. "Horses to ride and break in, if you want that kind of work for a change."

Bony pretended to consider. He was actually feeling doubt about the part he was playing, as though it were an inner voice warning him that loyalty could become a mastering force and, although misplaced, bring himself at odds with the principles which had guided him hitherto. Then doubt was banished by the thought: 'I am thinking as Nat Bonnay. I should be thinking as Inspector Bonaparte. I am Inspector Bonaparte; not Nat Bonnay the horse thief.'

He said: "I'd like to be a Conway."

CHAPTER 10

Surprises

THE FIRST of the winter fogs came two days after Bony
joined the Conways. Early in the afternoon, the sun lost its
power, and there appeared on the rim, eastward of the waterfall a frill, like wool. Midway down the slope a cloud formed
hung suspended there while its feet came downward as though
to seek a base. The mist along the rim came tumbling down
in great masses to join the lower cloud, swelling it swiftly and
increasing its descent until the settlement vanished and the
floor of Cork Valley appeared to be drawn into its chill em-
brace. For a few moments the sun was blue when it, too,
vanished.

Having no watch, Bony was unable to judge the time. He
worked on until, assessing the hour by the number of bags
filled with potatoes since the sun had disappeared, he decided
to return to the settlement before darkness and the fog made
the short journey hazardous even for so expert a bushman.

The fog was no hindrance. He negotiated the paddocks to
the lane by following his own pad, and once there merely continued along the rough track beside the river. He was barely
able to see the parallel fence beyond the stream. Eventually
the low bridge fording the river came out of the fog and he
was but three yards from it when he became aware of the
figure beyond it.

As any aborigine would do, Bony instinctively halted and
froze into a fire-blackened tree trunk. The person advanced,
and then turned off the track and down to the stream. Then
Bony could see it was a woman wearing a hooded raincoat.
She aroused his intense interest when, without sitting, she
removed her shoes and proceeded to cross the river, holding
to the side plank of the bridge to gain support on the slippery
boulders. At first he thought her mission was to find the screw-

driver, but she left the stream and put on her shoes. She came up the short bank to the track, and abruptly stopped when she saw him. She was Rosalie Conway. She said:

"Oh! It's you, Nat. You're early."

"Am I?"

"Whisper. Please. I thought I would meet you before you left the paddocks. I want to talk to you, Nat. Urgently."

Her eyes and her voice betrayed anxiety, and yet he sought duplicity and found no sign of it.

"Have you come to meet me . . . secretly?" Bony asked.

"Yes, yes. I want to ask you something, to get you to do something for me. But not just here. Someone could come along and find us."

A test! A trap! What was this? The awareness of danger, so quickly born in all wild things, and the aboriginal race so closely allied to them, now swayed this man who was half kin with them. His eyes blazed into the girl's dark eyes, flashed away to probe the surrounding fog for sign of an enemy. A full blood, he would have acted with resolution to maintain his assumed character; so much less than a full blood, the white man's impetuosity and the white man's reluctance to spurn the look of appeal in a pretty woman brought reason to clash with instinct, the gambler's passion to tussle with primitive intuition. He said:

"Why did you wade across the river, and not come by the bridge?"

As though impatient of the carefully worded question, Rosalie did two things at the same moment. She clutched Bony by the arm to urge him back from the bridge, at the same time answering his question.

"Because the bridge is wired to ring the buzzer at the house."

Decided now to give a little in return for that vital information, Bony suffered himself to be taken to the haven of a low bush from where he instantly saw that the track could be watched even in the fog. They sat, silently, while the girl regained her composure, and while he considered the implication of the wired bridge, and the probable answer as to why no one had surprised the people of Cork Valley. More a statement of fact than a query, he said:

"All the bridges are wired to give the alarm?"

"Yes." The girl bit her under-lip vexatiously. "I could have done wrong telling you about the bridge. But . . ."

"But . . ." he prompted, sharply.

"I could be making a terrible mistake about you," she said. "I've been watching you ever since you came. I've come to think you're a kind man at heart, and that you might do something for me, something I can't do for myself."

"I'm a Conway. As long as it isn't against the Conways."

"No. No, it isn't really." She hesitated for so long he thought she was waiting for him to speak, and purposely refrained. "All I want you to do is to post a letter for me."

"Why not post it yourself?"

"I can't do that here. You see . . ."

"I'm afraid I don't see. Why not be frank?"

"It's to a friend of mine. I . . . I don't want Mate to see it."

"How can I post it. Where?"

"You could give it to a girl who would post it in Kiama."

She was gazing steadily into his masked eyes, vainly seeking assurance, and he was on the defensive, alert to detect the trap.

"The day is passing," he reminded her. "It will be dark soon."

"Yes. Yes, I know. All right, I'll trust you, Nat. The letter is to a friend, and it's quite harmless to anyone here. You will be going away with the pack-horses in the morning, and at the end of the journey you will be met by a man with a truck, and his daughter, Bessie. All I want you to do is to give the letter to her. It's stamped and addressed. Bessie has been my friend always. She's posted a letter before. But don't let the others see you give the letter to her, will you? You mustn't do that."

"A love letter?" asked the romantic Bony.

Rosalie nodded, the admission emphasised by her eyes.

"The man I shall meet with the truck. Who is he? Describe him."

"His name's O'Grady. He's tall and thin. Bessie is tall, too.

73

She has fair hair and brown eyes, and she's one year younger than I am. Just give the letter to her without the others seeing . . ."

"Yes, you told me that. Where is the letter?"

Subjugating his interest in the journey with the horses to the immediate necessity of gaining further information concerning this 'illicit' posting, he said:

"I know your mother is the postmistress here, but you are old enough to write to whom you wish. Why should she not know about this?"

"Because . . . Well . . ." Rosalie hesitated. "Well Mate Conway isn't my mother. She's an aunt. I'm a Ryan, not a Conway. And besides, they want me to marry someone of their choosing and I'll not marry anyone I'm not in love with. You will do this for me, won't you?"

He accepted the letter and placed it in an inner pocket, doubting the wisdom of undertaking the errand although now convinced there was no subterfuge behind it. He was conscious of the deepening dusk, of the urgency of returning to the settlement, and the further urgency of pressing for more information.

"Oh, Nat, thank you," she said, enormous relief shining in her eyes. "Look, it's getting dark. We must hurry."

Together they walked to the bridge, which she said they would have to cross together, else the alarm would ring twice. She held his arm and told him to walk in step with her, and to place each foot on the same planks of the decking. On the far side, she said:

"Now they'll know that you have crossed on your way from work. Let me go first. Dawdle a little. And thank you, Nat. I can't say how grateful I am."

The fog took Rosalie Ryan, and then Bony remembered he wanted to ask how she knew about the journey he was to take with horses. Horses! Were they the strange horses that had appeared in Kelly's paddock, and had been shod, or re-shod in preparation for this journey? The bridges were wired to give notice of anyone crossing, of any car or truck! All bridges were wired to give the alarm, so the girl had said.

Interesting—very much so. On crossing the bridge, the domestic indicator in the living-room would inform the Conways that he had crossed. The indicator had told them when the car had come down the mountain track, the car that had gone on towards the waterfall without lights that night. Oh, yes, very interesting to Inspector Bonaparte.

Comment as dinner was being served revealed that his lateness hadn't gone unnoticed, and he countered this by explaining that as there was no sun to tell him the time, he had misjudged the time to leave work. After dinner, Mike Conway took him to what was evidently an office, where he was invited to sit and smoke.

"Want you to take a spell from spud digging for a couple of days, Nat. All right with you?" Mike Conway began.

"Yes, why not?" replied Bony easily. "What's doing?"

"There's produce to deliver to people in Kiama. Has to go by the back track. Rough track. Have to use horses, pack-horses."

Conway paused, and Bony was expected to say something.

"Sounds all right to me," he said. "I think I can use horses. Had plenty of experience with 'em, as you know."

Mike Conway gave one of his rare half smiles.

"The fellows with the horses are capable enough, Nat. Where you come in is your experience with horses under conditions which don't normally apply to Cork Valley. In addition, of course, to my summing up of you as a reliable man who could be depended on to have the Conway interests at heart."

"That's true, Mike."

"I feel sure it is. We do a fair bit of marketing by the back track, if you get me. We've never believed in paying more than we need to, and we believe in getting as much as possible for our produce. That means, of course, closing an eye to this and that. You understand?"

"Beginning to," replied Bony.

"We have to take risks, of course. However, normal precautions keep the risks down to a minimum. The returns are high, and we all share in the greater prosperity. With this job I'd like you to take on there are certain physical hardships, but as I've pointed out, the pay is exceptional."

"But not everything, I hope," observed Bony. "You know me, and I think I know you. You Conways have been generous. You've given me protection, and that sort of thing. We might get on faster if I could ask a question without giving offence."

"Ask away, Nat, ask away."

"Is this marketing by the back track illegal?"

"Well, in a way it is."

"It might be better if I don't know what your produce is," Bony said. "Let's keep to the actual job of getting the produce to the market. I'll do my part in that, Mike."

"Good!" exclaimed Conway. "As I said, the pay is . . ."

"And, as I said, the pay isn't everything. I don't forget that you Conways have taken me as a Conway. I'm happy enough with you. You've given me a square deal. I'll give you one."

"Good again, Nat. Well, the drill is this. I'll call you for breakfast at four in the morning. The horses and men will be ready to leave just before daybreak."

"Suits me," agreed Bony.

"By the way! I'll have your bagged spuds brought in, and the lot credited to you. Joe Flanagan said he'd had a few words with you about conditions here. Annual holiday, and that kind of thing. They earn plenty of money for a good annual. No one's expected to stay in Cork Valley without a bender outside. Okay?"

"Okay by me, Mike. Well, if I'm to be up at four, I think I'll turn in. Thanks, Mike, for everything."

So Rosalie Ryan had been right about this coming trip with the horses; and, not unnaturally, having studied potatoes for three weeks, the prospect of a change gave Bony an anticipatory thrill. There were to be mountains, and travel by horse, and produce which was illegal. Almost certainly smuggling!

Well, so what? His assignment didn't include 'Smuggling—Investigation of'. His assignment covered only 'Homicide'. The suspected murder of Excise Officer Torby might well be associated with smuggling, for illicit stills and suchlike were thought to be the motif of his walking tour at the time he was found . . . dead.

Smuggling! Smugglers! It sounded romantic. In the books he had read, the clever smugglers invariably outwitted the revenue officers, and the coastguards of a later era. What fights they had! What escapes from being hanged and suspended over the turnpikes until they rotted! The fortunes they made; especially those made by gentlemen of high estate who were granted knighthoods and had never experienced physical hardship.

Smuggling! Was it the right word to describe taking 'produce' out of a country? You smuggled something into a country. Could it be said you smuggled something out? This delicate point was occupying Bony's mind as he groped his way along the side of the shed to reach his cellar apartment. Fog is right. Well, smugglers always like fog to assist them in filling the secret wine bins and snuff jars of the lords and ladies.

Bony was obliged to feel his way round to the front of the shed. He couldn't see the houses, or the television antennae servicing the sets that didn't pay taxes. Down in the apartment it was appreciably warmer, and having lit the lamp, Bony sat and smoked, and silently chuckled.

The alarm clock said it was five to nine, and he was to be called at four in the morning. The bed invited, and he accepted the invitation. He began to undress, and then remembered the letter he was to post for Rosalie. Rosalie! A pretty name, indeed. A pretty owner of the name, too. The pocket of the coat had better be secured with a safety pin.

And then he was gazing down at the inscription in the neat handwriting, only obliquely conscious of the stamp affixed for the posting. It was addressed to Mr Eric Hillier, 10 Evian Street, Rose Bay, Sydney. How strange! Mr Eric Torby had lived at Number 10 Evian Street, Rose Bay.

CHAPTER 11

Out the Back Door

"IT's FOUR o'clock, Nat, and breakfast's ready," called Mike Conway down the trap-door steps.

Ten minutes later, Bony appeared in the living-room where Mike Conway had cooked breakfast of bacon and eggs, toast and coffee. The logs on the hearth fire had been replenished. The table was set at that end nearest the fire, and Mike nodded to the chair placed there.

"I'll explain the set up while you eat, Nat," he said, and also sat and sipped coffee. "On the chair over there is a roll of blankets in a ground sheet, and there's a military greatcoat as it will be cold, with leggings as well.

"Besides you, there will be three men. One of them you won't see by day. At least I hope not. He'll be young Brian Kelly, who will keep well ahead of you and act as the scout. He'll leave signs to be followed, and by that I mean he'll give you constantly the green light—or the red one. The two men will show you how to read the signs. I want you to be able to read them in the future, and also to take particular notice of the track for future trips. Understand?"

"Yes, that's clear enough, Mike."

"The journey will take you two days, and then you'll be met by a man with a truck. For our purposes his name is Timothy O'Grady. He is tall and rangy. Long nose and small brown eyes, with a slight cast in the left one. He'll check the produce on to his truck and you will see to it that he signs the form of receipt on the delivery note. I have it here in this envelope. Under no circumstances must you forget to have him sign for the stuff. And he'll deliver goods to you for which you must sign."

"That's plain enough," Bony said. "The two men with me —to be trusted?"

Mike Conway's singular half smile flickered about his mouth.

"One is a Kelly, the other is Steve Conway," he explained. "Both can read Brian's signs, but cannot read or write. Never went to school, and don't miss that. Both are good men. On the mountains and with horses."

"Can I ask a question?"

Mike nodded, brows raised enquiringly.

"Are they armed?"

"Only with their tongues," replied Mike. "They're expert with those. Don't worry. Everything is taken care of. I'll tell you this much, Nat. My great-grandfather started this trade something more than a hundred years ago, and there's never been a hitch. All down through the years the most important man on these trips has been the scout. You were born for that, Nat. It was why I picked you up that day. This trip you go with the horses. Next time you go with the scout. After that you will be the scout. You'll have the picture when you get back."

"All right, then I'm all set, Mike. Can I ask one more question?"

"Go ahead."

"You say Brian Kelly will be scouting on this trip. What's wrong with him scouting on the next and the next? Anything I should know?"

"Don't see why not," agreed Conway. "There are some who are born to scout over these mountains, and some who are born only to dig spuds. Brian took to scouting years before he went out to college. Did well at college. His father wants him to visit relatives in Ireland. Sending him over there for a year."

"He doesn't want to go?"

"He's not keen, Nat." Mike pursed his lips. Then he added: "We want him to go, Nat. He's inclined to be troublesome to our Rosalie, as a matter of fact. The change will give him new horizons, new interests. His boat sails in July."

"Oh!" Bony stood up. "Didn't mean to probe into family affairs. None of my business."

"It's the Conways' business. Remember you're a Conway. Well, here's the delivery note. And it's most important to get O'Grady's signature."

"I'll do that, Mike."

Wearing the military overcoat and carrying the blanket roll, Bony accompanied Mike Conway along the settlement roadway and on past the cheese factory. The fog was less dense, but the morning was cold and still dark. Conway carried a powerful torch which he directed to the ground just beyond their feet, so they could follow the rough track on to the piggery. This in turn was passed. The track led them to a low bridge spanning the river, and Bony wondered if this bridge, too, was wired.

He could hear the incessant noise of the waterfall some distant ahead and thought they were making for it when Conway took a divergent track which was nothing more than a path through close-skirting scrub. They followed this for perhaps a quarter mile when someone with a torch came from behind what proved to be a hut. Here the horses and several men were waiting. The man with the torch greeted them with:

"All set, Mike. Mornin', Nat! Give us your roll and I'll add it to a pack."

"Brian left?" asked Mike.

"Twenty minutes ago." He was one of those who ate at the Conway table, and Bony knew him as Steve. The blanket roll was strapped to the load on one of the vague shapes of horses. The second man appeared, and this one Bony didn't know. He said:

"Brian took Paddy and Tottie. Said that Streaky wasn't up to the mark. Said would you take her back some time. She's tied up over there."

"All right. Well, you'd better start. Good luck fellers."

The cavalcade moved off, each horse tethered to the pack of the one in front. The strange man led them and Steve, and Bony followed close behind the last. There was no wind, but the air was sharp, and it was so dark that Bony and his companion had almost to walk on the hind hooves of the animal in front. One of the horses nickered, but other than that there was no sound save the dull thud-thud of hooves on soft earth.

So this is why Mike Conway had stopped to pick up the wayfarer I had first passed and then, after seeing the man's face, had decided to give him a lift with the end view of making him a scout serving a smuggling party. Respect for Mike Conway grew in Bony, and a suspicion that the man had profound depths became a conviction.

Since Steve chose to be silent, Bony thought in retrospect of the hints and incidents, and his instinctive reaction to them, which had gone into the vetting of him by Mike Conway and his grandmother. The vetting had been progressively and carefully done, and he would be rash, indeed, to believe he was now rated one hundred per cent. Conway's admission that he had picked up the wayfarer to induct him into the profession of smuggling banished any credit for altruism which the unwary might have granted.

Bony was sure that he would continue to be subject to check. Much would depend on the report that Steve Conway would give of him on their return to Cork Valley, and, as Red Kelly would have pronounced the word, he would have to be ever 'carshious'. The statement that neither Steve nor his companion could read or write was certainly at odds in these days when others of the Conways and Kellys had been educated outside Cork Valley. To have him, the new man, sign for goods to be brought back would certainly give the Conways a hold over Nat Bonnay. It could not be said that Brian Kelly was unable to write his name to a form of receipt, and Brian was one of this party.

Despite his feeling that Rosalie had been motivated by the desire to contact a lover by side-stepping the normal postal link with Cork Valley, the letter he now carried could be a test of his loyalty to Conway, could well be a trap, and if this or any other trap closed about him his body might be found far beyond Casement's rabbit burrow.

Hillier was the name of the addressee. Eric Hillier, at Number 10 Evian Street, Rose Bay. Eric Torby had lived there, and the name Hillier had neither been mentioned by Casement, nor appeared in any report. It had to be borne in mind that the identity of the body found on the road to Bowral had been kept from the public. It was known only to the police, and to the person or persons associated with his death.

There was, however, the strong presumption that Torby had called himself Hillier, and in view of Rosalie's apparent anxiety to write and have her letter posted to Hillier, it could also be presumed that she was entirely ignorant of the death of Torby, alias Hillier. But could this presumption be accepted in respect of the Conways and the Kellys? They might well know of Eric Hillier's death and the conveyance of the body to a distant place on a road.

Bony was affronted by the thought he would have to read the letter, no matter what he decided to do with it when he met Bessie O'Grady. He could visualise in posting it what would result. It would be passed to the police by Eric Torby's landlady, and they would easily trace the writer to Cork Valley where every person was listed, and they would interrogate Rosalie without waiting for Inspector Bonaparte to reappear. On several counts, therefore, the letter he carried could be dynamite.

A love letter! Love takes time to generate. If Hillier was Eric Torby, then Torby had been in Cork Valley, and for some time.

He was cogitating thus when they passed close to the bulk of a house so large it must have been that owned by the Kellys. There were no lights from the house, but a light did come from another building which could be a dairy or milking shed.

Half an hour later, at six o'clock, the horses stopped, and the lead man came back to say that Bony should go with him as the track would be rough. Up past the horses, none of which was to be ridden, Bony was told to walk close to the lead man who said his name was Jack. Bony could see only that Jack was short and apparently fat.

Now the going was rough, a narrow path leading upward through dense scrub, turning and twisting about mountain shoulders, slithering down into gullies and across gurgling streams and up the far side and on and always twisting among the branches of scrub and bush. The fog-shrouded night often compelled Jack to direct his masked torch to the ground, but he did not use it unless it was necessary. Only the constant slope from the left down to the right told Bony they were ascending to the rim at the south-west arc of the amphitheatre. He walked on the inside and often felt rock when feeling his way through the bush, and he knew without seeing that on Jack's other side there was a precipice. That, no plainsman likes.

Eventually the darkness greyed, and still later he was able to see, through the fog, the round face of his companion and the black outlines of bush and scrub branches. It was after that that Jack said:

"How ya going?"

"Still have my eyes and no skin off my nose," responded Bony.

"Worse going down than coming up. Anyway, we're running true to time. You'll want to keep your hair on over the next bit."

They came to the foot of a vast wall of rock extending into the fog, and the fog was a blessing, for the path followed the base of a mountain face, and there was nothing but space on the outer side, space hidden but nonetheless menacing, space without height or depth. Here there were no trees, no bush, only stony rubble which gave way under foot, and which caused the horses often to scrabble madly to keep themselves against the wall. Here they found a short sapling, whittled of its bark, lying on the path.

Picking it up, Jack said:

"Brian's up ahead, Nat. On the job. How would you like to go this-away followin' an all-night beano?"

"I'd be dead sober time I arrived home," asserted Bony, at that moment moving with his back to the wall like a crab racing for its hole.

"Long way down. Takes the loose stones more'n a minute. I've listened to 'em."

"I like the fog, Jack."

"Ya, I always do. Fog's the poor man's friend." To the lead horse: "Come on up, you silly ole bastard. This ain't a skating rink. Ya, as I was sayin', fog's the poor man's friend. Only time the poor man can say he's free, free to thumb his nose at all and sundry and kiss me backside. Great life if you don't weaken."

Bony hoped he wouldn't weaken while edging round a granite shoulder which, he was positively sure, overhung a drop of ten thousand miles. He recalled seeing often these rock faces from the stable earth in which grew nice, homely spuds, and he wondered if the kookaburras were even then down there waiting for him.

As long as he didn't slip, they wouldn't be seeing him this day. Blessed be the fog.

The fog was blessed. It continued to hem them in from space, as they scrabbled and slid and poked their way across the chin of one rock face after another, until Jack turned into what appeared to be a cathedral, gloomy and ghostly and haunted by the hound of the Baskervilles.

The hound was a beagle. It came to meet them, its jaws slavering, its great sad eyes reflecting the light behind the party. It came to sniff about Bony's legs and when Bony spoke its tail wagged. Jack removed the strip of green cloth from the animal's collar, and the beagle turned and ran on and out of the opposite door of the cathedral.

CHAPTER 12

The Smugglers' Apprentice

THE MEN quickly checked the pack balance and the straps of every horse, and again Bony led with Jack, the rotund and cheerful smuggler.

"Brian sent the dog back to tell us with the green ribbon that the scenery don't hide no one but dinkum Irish." He chuckled. "Dinkum Irish nails us, Nat. Red Kelly was tellin' us your name for us true Irish."

"There's a mighty lot of Irish who aren't dinkum," reciprocated Bony. "How about all those bastards in the government?"

"Bloody rats," snorted Jack. "Same with them in the police. Same with the Customs, same with all gov'ment departments. To hell with 'em. All the bastards can think about is two things."

Horses' hooves clip-clopped on rock. The 'cathedral' walls fell apart and they were again in the open, climbing steeply up the side of a gully.

"What are the two things?" pressed Bony, and when Jack replied there was no smile behind his eyes.

"Well, one is a sort of mania to tax people, specially poor people. Can't wear nothing without its being taxed. Can't eat and drink nothing without being taxed. Taxes all the time. The other is forever filling their own pockets. Every time a new parliament sits first thing to do is raise their wages. But they're cunnin' bastards, you know. For every pound they raise their own wages they increases ten times their perks what they don't pay no income tax on. They get gold passes for everything. I wouldn't be surprised if they give themselves gold passes to get 'em into public lavatories so's they don't have to pay thrippence like us poor people."

"You could be right," heartily agreed Inspector Bonaparte. "But the police can't raise their own wages."

"Oh them!" The contempt in Jack's voice was genuine. They arrived at the top of the gully, reached the rim of the highland surrounding Cork Valley, rose up from the fog into the clear rays of the rising sun. To one side there was a small patch of scrub, and Jack hurried the horse train to it and there permitted the panting animals to spell.

"Bit of open country to cross," he said. "Got to keep a look-out for chance airyplanes. Let's take a decko."

Bony accompanied him to the edge of the scrub-patch, and wasn't interested in chance aeroplanes. He was standing on a plateau of broken grey rock crisscrossed by streaks of foot-high bush. Level with this plateau was the summit of the fog. They were standing on a large raft afloat on a sea of snow, a sea without ripples extending to all points of the compass, and larger blue-black masses like islands having small mountains on them.

The sun's rays were warm compared with the darkness of the fog from which the party had emerged. Bony opened his lungs to the air, the thought that to smoke would be gross insult to nature. Turning about he gazed over the concealed gully and had to use his imagination to create the picture of Cork Valley, the settlement and the paddocks, and the track up the hill slopes to the white house on the far side. But . . . no! There was the white house occupied by Conway's mother and his broken brother. Bony could just see its roof above the white walls darker than the field of fog.

With his telescope that invalid brother could see them across the five miles or so of flat fog. The house was to the north, the sun was rising south-of-east. There came from the white house four distinct flashes. Jack and Steve both witnessed the signal but offered no explanation and Bony did not seek one.

There was an island half a mile to the south and from the island rose a thin column of black smoke. Jack said:

"Right-oh me feller-me-lads."

He hauled on the lead rope and the horses moved forward after him and Bony across their 'raft' to its far side, and then went down into the fog like stepping into the sea. The chill air met them again, and soon they were pressing onward through low scrub in which the trees appeared as giants minus heads and arms.

An hour passed, or what Bony estimated to be an hour, and Jack tirelessly led on the string of pack-animals. He seemed to be impatient, often tugging at the lead rope, and now and then Steve at the rear could be heard urging the horses to a quicker pace.

Thereafter, Bony began to think that riding one of the horses would be preferable to this continuous trudging over an uneven wallabie-pad. Unused to mountains, the muscles of his thighs and calves began to complain. Imperceptibly the fog thinned, and the sun appeared as a faintly blue disc. The giants now had arms spread wide and heads of massive foliage, and not long after he saw that the blue of the sun had changed to gold, and the trees and the bush and the rocks took on pastel tints. Somewhere to the left he could hear water singing a ceaseless song, and heard, too, the cackling laughter of kookaburras, and the harsh cries of the jays.

He was surprised to see a fern tree, and later the ropes of a climber about a tree. Now they must be travelling through a gorge wide and deep beneath those upper rafts and islands he had admired early in the morning.

For the third time a dog appeared, and not the same beagle this time. There was a green ribbon tied to collar—the green light to proceed—and when the ribbon had been removed by Jack, the dog wagged his tail and trotted on ahead, nose to the ground, to catch up with Brian Kelly scouting beyond sight of the party.

"Them dogs work out wide of young Brian," Jack explained. "Great snifters. Snift a stranger, or anyone, a mile off. Funny what you can do with dogs. You can even teach 'em never to bay, no matter what."

"They're better on the hoof than I am," Bony confessed, and the rotund man grinned as though to tire a half-abo plainsman was an achievement.

"You gotta train, Nat. You'll harden up. Anyway, we'll be spelling soon."

Half an hour later they did, after walking straight through a wall of scrub into a great open-mouthed cave. The lathered animals gave proof of the pace adopted by the men. The packs were removed and then Bony could see that one animal carried two bags of chaff, and another blanket-rolls and saddle bags which contained food.

A fire was lit and tea brewed. While the horses munched chaff from canvas nose-bags, they ate cold pickled pork and bread and butter and drank strong tea, Steve and Jack occasionally taking a sip of 'wine' to keep out the cold. Bony was glad to relax, sitting on his folded overcoat and resting his back against a partially filled sack of chaff.

The scene could have been staged, for it contained stagy characters, feeding horses, gear and merchandise.

It was more than presumption that they were engaged in an illegal traffic. Well, when there is profit in a trade, illegal or not, there are men ever ready to engage in it. What Bony could not as yet clearly understand was their mental attitude —shared by Red Kelly—to Irishmen in government and police, for in demeanour and words they had shown distinct hostility which sign-posted a schism among the Irish transplanted to Australia. It was deeper than the normal Irishry.

Another angle bothered him. The customary single-mindedness with which he tackled a criminal was being reduced through attacks made on his own weaknesses. Despite the recently disclosed reason why Mike Conway had picked him up and brought him to Cork Valley, there was no blinking aside that all the Conways had treated him, a confessed horse-thief, with unusual kindness, an attribute which must spring from a deeper motive than training him as a scout for their smuggling expeditions. The foundation on which he had built a most successful career was being undermined by this liking of people whom he ought to regard with cold antipathy since probably among them were ruthless murderers.

Bony rolled a cigarette, stretched his legs luxuriously, and marvelled at himself for actually thinking: 'Well, why be perturbed about such a problem, full of meat and tea in this cool cave and amid such a homely scene and people?' And then there was a beagle dog looking at him, and attached to the animal's collar was a piece of paper tied with a strip of red cloth.

"Tottie! Here, Tottie."

Bony looked towards Jack who had spoken and Jack was a changed man, no longer of cheerful mien. He was now deliberate in action as he untied the ribbon and released the paper. "Writin' on it, Steve. Brian knows we can't read writin'."

"He knows I can," Bony said. The men gazed at him, the little man suspiciously, the lank Steve with hope. "Pass it over." Still Jack hesitated, and there was an edge in Bony's voice when he said: "You said red on the dog's collar meant danger. The message tells what danger and where. Pass over that paper, Jack."

They were surprised by the undertones of command, and for an instant looked at him as though seeing him for the first time. He was still reclining against the bag of chaff, and Jack came forward on his hands and knees to surrender the paper. Bony read out the message.

" 'Two men following you. They just crossed Flood's Gap. Take the water track. Better hurry!' "

"Crikey, yes! Come on. Load up and get," snapped Steve, and they sprang to the job of repacking.

"How far back's Flood's Gap?" demanded Bony, almost tossing a pack saddle across the back of a horse, and not pausing for an answer.

"Half a mile," replied Jack. "Get on, hurry. We got to be well up the water track before they can catch up . . . if they're after us."

"After us, all right," snarled Steve, and Bony sought further information as he slung sack-protected bundles on to the saddle, and felt rather than heard the gug-guggle of liquid within.

"How far ahead is the water track? Tell me. Describe the road. I'll have to wait about here and trick 'em somehow. Then I'll overhaul you."

"Bit under a half-mile on you come to a shallow stream with

a wide sandy bottom. We follow the stream up for a quarter-mile to a fork. We take the right stream. Until we get to the fork we're wide open for them fellers to see us, and which stream we take from there. We follow that right stream for nigh on a mile, and leave it at a flat rock covering an acre or two."

"And after that?"

"You want to know a lot, Nat, don't you?" queried Jack, and Bony now panting under the strain caused by necessary haste, sneered:

"Hell of a good set-up, eh? Wandering about and leaving horse tracks for a blind man to follow with the tip of his stick. What sort of turn-out is this? And you arguing the bloody toss at a time when the demons are on our heels. Get going with these lumps of cat's meat. Get some steam out of 'em."

"All right . . . all right. But you ain't the boss," rebelled the fat man, and now Steve broke in.

" 'Bout time he was. I knew this track was too risky. Said so to Red and Brian. Never liked it. Come on you!" He grabbed the lead of the front horse, and the others urged the train into a frantic walk out through the screen of bush and into the sunlight of the wide-floored gorge.

Here Bony paused to look back and down. He could see nothing moving among the dotting boulders and the low bush and tall iron-barks. But he inwardly shuddered at the crass stupidity revealed by the plain trail of horse tracks, going back and down to the reported trackers, and continuing upward after the hurrying pack train.

For a little way he followed the train, running from tree to tree, visually searching the rear from each tree, and eventually the train disappeared ahead, and he waited in the shelter of several hillside boulders to gain sight of the followers. A few minutes after that they appeared.

They were following the horse trail, plain enough for a city pavement walker to follow. They carried equipment on their backs and were dressed in the stout clothes of the bushwalker, the city fellow who delights in spending his holidays and weekends in tramping through the mountains à la senior boy scout.

The more experienced are truly expert, and most of them belong to a club or organisation.

These two men Bony was now watching were equipped to spend days and nights in the mountains, and it was obvious that they were physically fit to carry their equipment. He recognised them. They were the two who had crossed Red Kelly's paddocks. Now they were walking steadily up the gorge, eyes on the tracks and Bony waited for them to see the tracks turning off into the scrub masking the cave. Here they halted, and their actions proclaimed them to be experienced bushmen. They spent less than half a minute there, and again proceeded up the gorge.

Their interest gave Bony the opportunity to slip away from the boulders, and he ran on after the horse train, seeking means by which he could delay the pursuers. The slopes of the gorge abruptly drew close and became exceedingly steep, forming a natural gateway to a much wider one crossing it, like the top bar of the letter T.

From the gateway Bony could see the horse train splashing its way along the bed of a stream which came down from the right, and now there was no doubt that the bushwalkers would arrive at this place before the train could reach a spur at the junction of two lesser streams. Bony saw how they could be delayed—if there was time left to him.

Unencumbered by the heavy overcoat he had packed on a horse, he raced back into the 'gateway' and climbed the right slope, pulling his felt hat forward, and knotting a handkerchief about his nose and mouth in the approved style of the hold-up thug. From a hundred feet up he could see the two men, still in the wider section of the gorge. He was sobbing for breath after climbing two hundred feet, and here, as previously observed, there was a wide ledge thickly littered with boulders, ranging from a ton to several pounds, which had fallen from the higher slope.

He shouted. The men looked up, saw him, stopped. One raised a pair of slung binoculars to his eyes, and Bony thumbed his nose. Halted, they conferred, and Bony gained two minutes. Then they came on with that steady pace which tells of trained leg muscles. They stopped again when Bony toppled over the ledge a boulder weighing a hundred odd pounds, and they watched the boulder falling and bouncing and smashing its way down to the horse trail they were following. They watched a second boulder smashing down to thud on the trail closer to them, and the third which thudded still closer. The retreat began when the fourth boulder loomed like a sputnik over their heads.

CHAPTER 13

No Guns for Smugglers

THE STREAM averaged ten feet in width and was seldom more than a foot deep. The water was icy cold and crystal clear, and the grey sandy bottom was ribbed and ceaselessly in movement.

At the place where the pack train reached the water the hills were swept back to form a narrow valley; the floor covered with coarse grass, the slopes massed with buttresses of rock and robust trees.

The men urged the horses to frantic effort, accepting the risk that a load might slip under a horse's belly. The animals splashed themselves, their packs and both men, and rear-man Steve shouted to them, waved a stick and ploughed after the rearmost horse despite the constant shower of water thrown up by their hooves.

Steve was furiously angry, but not by the water, which was incidental. He was an easy going man, prone to give way early in any argument. He had voiced his objection to this track, but had not pressed it against the decision reached by Red Kelly and his son. They depended on the fog's continuance. He had countered that early in the season the fog cannot be relied on.

The plan had been to reach the cave behind the scrub screen before, or at least soon after, the sun thinned the fog to a light mist, even dispelled it. They were to stay there, fog or no fog, until night fell again and then proceed to the valley, and take a zig-zag track up the opposite slope. The first part of the journey, from Cork Valley to the cave, was thought to be comparatively safe when the fog was thick, and bushwalkers and others don't usually walk about these mountains.

Now it was essential to take a dangerous cross-track to an alternative track by which they could reach O'Grady and his truck.

Steve was experiencing the nightmarish effort of trying to run in leaden boots. For what seemed an hour they were right out in the open and in clear sunlight, and constantly he looked back, expecting to see the two followers in the valley behind them. Unable to see Bony, Steve thought of treachery, and swiftly reviewed all the early reservations they had had about this stranger who had come to Cork Valley. The suspicion that he was a police spy returned, and he could see nothing ahead but disaster following his surrender to the views of the Kellys.

The Kellys always shouted and bashed their way through life; the Conways used their brains and spoke softly.

The junction of the two streams was eventually reached, and Jack took the right one which became narrow and deeper but still sandy. Almost at once the hills closed in tight and concealed them from the valley, and Steve paused to peer back from a tree and received renewed hope when he saw nothing that moved, not even Nat Bonnay.

He signalled to Jack that all was clear at the rear, and the train leader reduced the pace. Keeping to the stream, they proceeded for half an hour when the bottom became rocky and they were forced to turn up from it to a large area of rock. Here they left what was now a gully and moved into a still sharper gully rising steeply to the south.

An hour later, horses and men were scrabbling up rock steps to enter a veritable maze of gigantic boulders which once had been the core of an alp. Behind one of these rock masses stepped Brian Kelly.

He was dressed much like the bushwalkers, but he carried only a lightly-filled rucksack, and slung from a shoulder were powerful binoculars and strapped to his leather belt was a pistol holster, too large for the weapon concealed there.

"Nice how d'you do!" snarled Jack, and Steve grinned his anger and said not a word. "We better camp here."

Brian nodded and assisted them to remove loads and saddles. When the horses were tethered to a rope, the young man spoke for the first time.

"Could have been worse. Would have been worse if it hadn't been for Nat."

"How so?" asked Jack, leaning against a rock and opening a flat tin of tobacco. "Me and Steve's wetted to the skin 'cos we had to take to the stream. Me matches are soaked. Papers would have been, too, if they wasn't in the tin."

Brian handed him a box of matches. The dogs lay at his feet. The exhausted horses drooped; the sun was westering. Steve said:

"Nat musta been bushed trying to catch up. Or something."

"Or something, I'd say," Brian said, and laughed. "I saw you come out into Long Valley. I saw you reach the stream and begin to walk up it, and knew you'd take this track. I waited to see Nat. And d'you know where I did see him? He was climbing up the side of the gorge to that ledge. He was wearing something white over his face. When he got there he sort of saluted, and then began to roll rocks off the ledge. I could see the rocks going over."

"Pounding those fellers with rocks, eh?" Jack laughed but there was no humour in his eyes. "Good for Nat. He's shaping well."

"Could you see what they looked like?" Jack asked and Brian shook his head. "Too far when I saw them coming over Flood's Gap. Loaded up like bushwalkers."

"How do you know they were followin' us?" queried the lanky Steve.

"Couldn't be sure, and couldn't take a chance they were not."

"No, that's right," Steve agreed. "Anyway, it's a mess. If Nat has killed 'em there's going to be trouble of some sort. Mike isn't going to like it."

"Well, it couldn't be helped, could it?" flared Brian, and Steve exploded as quiet men sometimes do.

" 'Course it could be helped. We had no business coming this way for a start. I said so, but you and Red wouldn't listen. You know everything, or think you do, and you know nothing. Your old man made a mistake nine years back, and it stopped the trade for the rest of the season."

"I know nothing about that," Brian returned heatedly.

"That'll be enough, you two. Brian, you go back down the

track a bit and locate Nat. Me and Steve has to get ourselves dry."

Brian Kelly stood, fire in his eyes and a scowl ageing him. He snapped the fingers of his right hand, and a hound trotted off that way. He snapped the fingers of the other hand and the other dog loped off to that side. A moment later he had vanished among the great rocks.

With a dog working wide on either flank, he walked swiftly down the hillside track, and the track kept always to the screen of scrub and avoided open places. And he hadn't travelled far when halted by a voice behind him.

"Going back to Cork Valley, Brian?"

Spinning about, he saw Bony leaning against a track-side tree.

"Hell no! I didn't see you."

"You weren't meant to. How far on are the others?"

"Less than half a mile." Brian whistled softly. "Don't get it. The dogs missed you, too."

"They know my smell."

The dogs appeared, wagged tails at Bony, then followed the two men walking in single file up the sloping track.

"Did you kill those fellows? I saw you heaving rocks down on them."

"I fixed 'em," boasted Bony. "Tell you about it when we catch up."

The men had a blazing fire of well dried wood giving but little smoke. They were standing close and both were enveloped by steam for they had removed none of their clothes. Both were decidedly anxious to have Bony's story.

"I think they were the two that Red stopped crossing the valley," Bony began. "I'm not sure, though. Got up like bush-walkers, but tougher than I'd imagine ordinary city hikers. I had to stop them before they got into that valley when they would have seen you walking up stream."

"I saw you heaving rocks down on them," Brian claimed.

"I had to do something, as I said. I rolled a boulder down about a hundred yards in front of them. Then another, closer. And another and another still closer. They got the idea. They went off, fast, and I sneaked down off the ledge without them seeing me, and got into the valley and headed down stream. It took them the best part of half an hour to come out of that bottle-neck and then I let them catch a glimpse of me as though not intending to. They were given another idea. They thought we went down stream. I watched them walk to the stream, look at it, talk about it, and then they walked one on either side . . . down stream."

Steve was smiling. Jack was grinning happily. Brian was openly admiring.

"So you didn't kill 'em. Good for you, Nat," exclaimed the rotund smuggler.

Bony frowned, his blue eyes widened and stared at each in turn.

"Kill 'em!" he echoed. "Kill them! Think we want the police all over the country? Think we want . . . What the hell d'you take me for? What is this? I don't get it. I'm not having anything to do with murder. And you . . . " he pointed at the holster on Brian's belt. "What have you got in that. A gun?"

"Well, it isn't a plug of tobacco."

The four men became immobile. Brian Kelly stood with feet apart and hands lightly pressed into his broad hips. Steve and Jack moved only their eyes, and those but fractionally. Bony looked upward from the pistol holster to the grey eyes flaring defiantly, clearly aware that he was to have that weapon firstly to cement his standing with the Conways, and secondly to banish the possibility of himself being associated with homicide—on the wrong side. His voice was low but heard.

"I was given a job by Mike Conway. I was told to deliver goods to a man named O'Grady, and to take other goods from O'Grady. I don't know the nature of the goods, and I'm not asking. I do know we're engaged in unlawful trade, and that doesn't bother me. I am not having anything to do with a trade when concealable arms add another three years to a five-year sentence, and a life sentence if a killing is done. You hand me that pistol or I'll cripple you."

"Come and get it," invited the son of Red Kelly.

Bony began the short walk, and Steve said:

"Wait on, Nat. Brian, what happened to Ted Kelso could happen to you. It's one for all and all for one. You've been brought up on that. It was fed to you from your mother's breast. The rule is no firearms on this job. Hand it over."

Kelly looked from Steve to Bony, and from Bony to Jack. His eyes were minus that candidness which had appealed to Bony at their first meeting. Steve's hazel eyes and Jack's eyes, now hard as agates, he found less trying than the blue eyes which seemed to have the piercing property of a searchlight. Slowly Brian removed the belt, slipped the holster from it, dropped the holster to the ground and replaced the belt. The pistol in the holster Bony dropped into a deep crevice in the rock floor.

"Now we can breathe again," he told them. "If we can't do a spot of smuggling without guns, we'd better go home. You've been among these mountains all your lives. I've been in them only about ten minutes, and you've made mistake on mistake. In half an hour the fog will be back. You tell me what's ahead because I'm running no risks of going to gaol."

CHAPTER 14

Fog Can Be a Friend

THE FOG rolled up the ravines and gullies, and it lapped distant ridges as great white waves breaking on a rock-girt coast.

The smugglers decided to push on and take advantage of the remaining daylight. Brian Kelly and his dogs disappeared when the packing was begun, and this time the chore was efficiently accomplished.

Bony was well pleased by the victory over Brian Kelly which, following the outwitting of the two bushwalking types, would surely gain for him one hundred per cent of confidence by the men of Cork Valley. Also he was feeling that this smuggling trip was to be the turning point which came sooner or later in those of his assignments he had to tackle in the guise of an itinerant character. In this he excelled because he had the patience and the ability to ingratiate himself among those to be courted.

Usually crime investigation is conducted by an organisation against an individual but sometimes conditions call for action by an individual against an organisation. Such conditions were thought to exist in these southern mountains of New South Wales, and the lone investigator had first to be received by the members of the suspected organisation. This Bony had done, and now was proving to his own satisfaction that the suspected organisation was true in fact.

Inheriting the patience of the most patient race on earth, he was ever impatient with official interference, and often defiant of official recall. He had been careful to stress to Superintendent Casement that the assignment was to be uncluttered by any attempt to supervise him, any action which would create frustration and additional hazards. Casement had agreed to keep clear, and Bony thought it was unlikely that the superintendent of this vast land area would annul the arrangement.

He could not, however, be as sure of the sub-section of the Customs Department who would continue to take vital interest in the murder of Excise Officer Torby. Thus his victory over the two bushwalkers provided not a little joy, as well as pleasant prod to his vanity. And finally who the heck did the Customs Department think it was that it could poach on the preserves of the Police Department?

Pistols, however, could not be tolerated, and in this matter the Conways were one with him.

There was mention of a man named Kelso, and, not long before the name Kelso was spoken, there was mention of an affair of nine years ago. Quite by accident, Bony had arrived at the rock halt within minutes of the pack train, and he had overheard Steve's frank criticism of the Kellys' decision to send the train this way. Steve then had said: "Your old man made a mistake nine years back, and it stopped the trade for the rest of the season." And then, during the incident of the pistol, Steve had said: "What happened to Ted Kelso could happen to you. It's one for all and all for one."

Some time in the night, they passed from the fog into blackness and Jack's torch revealed the waiting Brian as well as the walls of a vast cave. Jack said they would be camping here for the remainder of the night and probably the following day, as a deal of scouting would have to be done before the final stage could be attempted.

After a meal of cold meat and hot tea, and a 'snort' of the Conways' 'white wine'. Bony was indeed happy to spread his blankets on the sandy floor of this huge cave, and sink into sleep, warmed by the large fire. He woke refreshed, the muscular ache in his legs gone. The fire was a mound of red coals, and the others still slept.

Brian Kelly was the next to stir. He found Bony squatting on his heels before the replenished fire, the light of which revealed only one sectional wall of the cave.

"How's things?" he asked, helping himself to a mug of coffee. "Crikey, how I needed that sleep."

"I, too," admitted Bony. "No bad feelings this morning?"

"Don't last long with me." Brian sipped from the mug. "Of course, we could strip down and have a real go. If you feel like it."

"I don't feel like it."

"Early, I'll agree." Brian emptied his mug and refilled it. He crammed tobacco into his pipe and applied a fiery stick to it. "How are you liking his kind of work?"

"Change from digging spuds."

"Could be more dough in it, too. Anyway, you'll have enough of it, although, mind you, getting away from the settlement has its points. I'll be away from it in a few weeks for a long time. They tell you about it?"

"Mike did say something about you going off on a trip overseas," Bony replied casually. "Been away before?"

"No, and I'm not keen to go now. You been outside the country?"

Bony shook his head negatively. He said: "I never had enough money."

"No one ever has . . . legally." Brian stared moodily at the fire. There's a Kelly in a shipping office up in Sydney. Comes home sometimes. He says that only five per cent of first-class travellers going overseas pay their own fares. Says the other ninety-five per cent have their fares paid by the tax-payers. They're just bots. Politicians and top civil servants and marketing-board people. You pay taxes?"

"Not more than I can help," replied Bony.

"Same with me . . ." Brian grinned. "And I'm out to get back all I can get of what the bastards take from me."

Bony chuckled saying: "Would you have to go your hardest to do that?"

"Well, a feller's got to make a profit on the deal, hasn't he?"

"Your passage booked yet?"

"Yes, I'm leaving on July 28. Going to London, and over to Dublin. Anyway, I'll be here for the festival. That'll stir your blood, Nat."

"Cork Valley Festival?" pressed the interested Bony.

"Yes. Everyone has a festival these days. Jacaranda Festival up in Grafton. Festival of Flowers over in Bowral. Pea Festival at Markham. Cork Valley Festival. Ours is a bit private like. Only relations and close friends permitted."

"Sounds interesting."

"She warms up in the evening," Brian smiled broadly, and glanced at his watch. "Hell, it's ten to nine! I must get on to the job. Kick those sleeping loafers to life while I have a wash and get on with breakfast."

He seemed to have no inhibitions. Stripping off by the fire, he crossed to the rock-guttered stream bisecting the floor of the cave and splashed its icy water over his powerful body. Jack fed the tethered horses, and Steve contented himself with washing his hands before placing a couple of dozen mutton chops to grill on a spread of wire netting. Bony couldn't face an icy bath and washed only his face and hands, Jack did likewise. The freed dogs joined them to crunch the chop bones.

"What d'you reckon?" Jack asked Steve. "Think we oughta do the razorback?"

"Safest," replied the lank man. "No more chances."

"Best, I suppose, as we don't know just where those flaming bushwalkers could be. Will you stay back, or is it me?"

"I'll stay," Steve decided.

"All right! You take the hounds, Brian. I'll give you half an hour start, and you wait for me at O'Grady's top gate. Before I forget, or you do, I'll get those coloured rags for the dogs." Jack brought the rags he had taken from the dogs' collars the previous day, and Bony learned by watching both men preparing a lunch that they expected to be away most of the day. When Brian had left, the rotund Jack rejoined Steve and Bony at the fire.

"Think you could find your way back to Cork Valley?" he asked of Bony, and, faintly amused, Bony replied:

"Put a cat in a bag, take him a dozen miles away, and the cat will go home. The cat's mind registered every twist and turn when in the bag. My mind did just that in the fog and the dark."

Steve sighed, and Jack looked his admiration.

"I believe you could. All the way back to the Valley," Jack said. "What say you back-track for about two miles. You'll come to a razorback joining two mountains. Up to the left is a high tor. From there you could keep an eye on the razor-back, and see as far as that stream we ploughed through yester-day. Stay there till just before sundown. How's that?"

"Clear enough," agreed Bony. "And if I see those spies I come back here?"

"That's the idea . . . if you can't trick 'em like you did before." Jack laughed. "I'll take two of the horses and make a false trail past this place. You take some grub, Nat."

Jack fashioned a saddle with his blanket-roll, and rode off down a rock passage, leading the second horse with a bridle rope. Reminded of Don Quixote, Bony followed on foot, and they entered bright sunlight flooding a narrow gorge. Jack, perched on his horse, rode off a shelf of rock to normal ground where the pack train had left it for the rock shelf, and there pro-ceeded on past the turn-off to give continuity to the horse tracks

Bony followed back the tracks made the previous night. They were so plain that no average bushman would be faulted, and much could have been done to wipe them out at places and cause confusion. He wondered if it was mere Irishry, the supreme confidence in a scout working ahead, and scorn of taking precautions against being trailed.

At one place he concealed himself behind a rock and smoked two cigarettes, making sure Steve was not following him as a check, and when reasonably sure that he wasn't followed, he went on down the trail till he came to the tor, a little alp of rocks piled on top of one another, on the summit of a bald hill.

From the tor none could complain of the scenery in any direction. To the north was the razorback, a wall of some five hundred yards in length and joining the sheer slope of one mountain with that of another. The top of the wall was often reduced to about five feet in width, and was never less than three hundred feet from its base. Bony's feet tingled at the memory of crossing it in the dark of night.

Now lounging among the rough boulders comprising the tor, Bony could gaze across ridge beyond ridge in all directions and down into valleys where water lay in silvered threads. The entire country comprised jump-ups, chasms, gorges and gullies, and he was further convinced that the two bushwalkers were equally as expert in this land as the men of Cork Valley.

They could not be normal city-loving people on a walking tour.

Trails of mist in the deeper levels were a reminder of last night's fog and spoke of another which would come again soon after the sun set, and might rise much earlier. The morning passed without a sign of a human being. He watched the high-flying eagles, and doubtless they watched him. The crows were scarce, although one did investigate him before flying off. A cardinal-hatted Australian robin amused him, and once he glimpsed a stag deer on a crag.

He had brought water in a billy can for another purpose besides making tea for lunch, and having gathered dry sticks on the way, he lit a small fire and heated the water. When it was boiling, he held Rosalie Ryan's letter to Eric Hillier in the steam. It was not difficult to raise the flap of the envelope with the blade of a knife. He read:

DEAR ERIC,

I am sending this letter by two friends, one of whom will pass it to another who will post it in Kiama. I have waited so long for a letter from you that I wonder if Mate Conway stopped it at the Office here. I would have written to you had I your address, and you will remember how suddenly you left Cork Valley. It was only the other day that quite by chance I came across it in the book I lent you, and found your note in which you wrote those wonderful words. And there at the beginning was your address.

Dear Eric, do please write to me and say you meant those words. Please send your letter to Miss M. Mathews, Care of the Post Office, Bowral, and add 'to be called for'. I am to go to Bowral in ten days to buy a few things for our Festival, and I will manage to go into the Post Office without being seen. You must know how difficult it is for me here.

When I found your message in the book and read that you adored me and would come back some day and claim me for your wife, I just cried with happiness. So do please, please, dear Eric, write to me at once so that I can get it at the Bowral Post Office

Reluctantly Bony burnt the letter, and in the envelope enclosed a note for Superintendent Casement.

A Recruit for the Rebels

ON THE sun going down beyond the welter of ridges Bony left the tor, and all the way back to the great cave he made sure he hadn't been tracked by Steve. Both Jack and Brian Kelly were there before him, and all were interested to have his report.

"As you said this morning," Bony began, "from that tor the stream you walked in can be seen. I wished I had glasses. I saw two men walking up stream about four o'clock. I don't think they were carrying packs. They halted at the junction of the two streams, and poked about there for twenty minutes. Then they walked down stream again. They're probably camped some distance down stream."

"Blast 'em!" snapped Jack, and Bony argued.

"Better behind us than ahead of us. The way ahead is clear, I take it."

"Yes," Brian replied for the fat man.

"Then why worry? There's no one to interfere with delivery to Mister O'Grady. On the way back we'll have those fellers ahead of us, and if we can't pass them we'll have to slip round them. No difficulty there."

"No dice, Nat. We don't go back this way," declared Jack, and Steve agreed with him.

"Not with the back loading we'll have," interjected Brian.

"There'll be no back loading either," Jack asserted.

"What's wrong with the back loading? Dynamite?"

"No, Nat. Only sugar," replied Brian, and Steve, who was grilling steaks, quietly cut in with:

"We don't take the back loading. Now, let's eat and get on with the job in hand."

Sugar! Sugar is used in the distillation of spirits, and because of the risk that Mike Conway might be stopped and his truck searched, sugar had to be smuggled in by the back way, to supplement the small surplus above ordinary community use. And so by the story about the two men camped on the stream, Bony had hindered the trade in Mountain Dew, and hoped to learn of another track over these mountains between Cork Valley and O'Grady.

"Mike tell you we were to meet O'Grady with his truck?"

"Yes, and that I am to get his receipt for the forward loading and give ours for the back loading," replied Bony in answer to Jack's question.

"Well, gettin' chased by those two fellers makes us take on another plan. We don't deliver to O'Grady's truck, but to a barn he's got at the back of his farm. The track's clear, and I seen O'Grady today and arranged it. Takes more time, but that can't be helped. Get that?"

"Of course."

"At the place we'll tell you about, we'll bypass Brian and the dogs. He'll stay there until we leave the barn, and then he'll be ahead of us on the way back. How's that?"

"Good as far as it goes," replied Bony. "But when I'm on this job I'm having a scout behind me as well as in front."

"Argue that out with Red, Nat."

"No trouble, Jack," Bony airily assured him. "Now about that sugar we take back."

The little fat man laughed outright, saying to the others:

"Ain't he a beaut? He should of been a pirate, eh? He's born to it, ain't he?" Then to Bony: "Nat, me bhoy, you does just what you're told, and me and Steve is telling you. O'Grady will be tellin' you, too. And he has the sugar. Don't be worrying so. We'll have some back loading. And with that, we go home by another track."

"All right, but don't say I was nervous about handling a few bags of sugar for the kids at the valley."

That raised another chuckle from Jack, and Steve laughed in his dry manner.

It was dusk when they left the great cave, with Brian and the dogs again well in the lead. This evening the fog was absent, and all the slopes were lustrous green at the base and purple velvet at the summit. When night came the slopes were discernible only by their emptiness of star points.

A dog stopped them after something more than an hour, and Jack's torch showed a green rag tied to its collar. As hitherto, when the rag was removed the dog at once loped away to follow Brian Kelly. Another hour followed and then they came out on to what was obviously a shelf overlooking the coast lowlands. Jack said this was where they would spell the horses for half an hour. He said, too, that the lights far away to the left were those of Kiama, and that the glow in the sky to the south marked Nowra, a moderate sized town.

"We'll come back from O'Grady's as far as this place," he explained. "We'll go direct inland, which is why Brian will wait here instead of going with us to the barn."

They lapsed into silence, and when Bony was beginning to wonder when they would go on, as Jack's half hour was nearing a full hour, he detected a faint sound and saw a shadowy figure just beyond the temporary camp. It was silhouetted by the glow of Nowra's lights, and he knew it wasn't Brian Kelly.

Silently he stood, and silently he advanced to the figure. It came on stealthily, failed to see him, and then was seized and held by an arm lock.

"Damn you, let me go!"

"Ah! So it's a woman. Now who are you?" demanded Bony, and Jack chuckled and answered for her.

"She's our Bessie O'Grady, Nat. Let her be."

Bessie was almost as tall as Bony, and certainly capable. Releasing her he was only just in time to avoid a blow at his face and would not have escaped if Nowra's kindly sky-glow hadn't revealed her raised arm.

"Now now! No offence meant," he chided. "No one told me you were expected. Now don't be rough. I'm apologising."

"Damn you, you nearly broke my arm," the girl hissed, for it wasn't the time or place to shout. "Who the hell are you, anyway?"

"He's Nat Bonnay," Jack again replied for Bony. "Cork Valley bloke. I told your dad about him when I was over."

"Didn't tell me about him. All right, you Nat Bonnay. I'll

let up this time, but don't you ever grab me no more."

"Not without invitation, Bessie," Bony said.

"It'll be a long time before you get that. Well, do we stay all night?"

The pack train moved off with Bony and the girl and Jack in the lead. They skirted a cliff and then descended by a gully to an invisible track which twisted and turned interminably. Wondering why the girl had met them at a spot far outside the boundary of her father's farm, he probed.

"I've to take you in by a new track," she told him. "Dad ain't so good in the dark. His eyes are going on him. How old are you, Nat?"

"Old!" The question startled him. "Well, now, I could be thirty and I could be fifty. It depends."

"Married?"

"My eyes see only Rosalie."

"Oh!" Bessie said nothing more for five minutes. She gained Bony's admiration for her sure-footedness and supreme confidence in the darkness. "Might be hard to get, Nat."

"Only teasing. I wouldn't have a chance."

"I'll tell you my opinion when I see you in the light."

First it was soft ground, then it was rock, and presently it became shingle indicating to Bony that they were following the dry bed of a stream. He asked:

"Are you married?"

"No. But I'm going to be."

"Who's the feller?" questioned Jack. "Can't be me. Or is it?"

"What d'you think? I'll tell you who, so you won't have no disappointments. It's Brian Kelly. He doesn't know it yet, but he will in proper time. He thinks he's catching up on Rosalie, but me and Rosalie are planning it different."

"You're great friends?" pressed Bony, still undecided what to do about the mission entrusted to him.

"Rosalie's the only friend I've got, exceptin' Dad. I'd do anything for Rosalie, anything. I'd kill that Brian Kelly, or anyone else who crossed her up. So you take care, Nat."

They came to a gate, which Bessie opened and stayed to shut

after the train. When it was apparent that Jack knew the track from here on and the girl must be walking with Steve, Bony put another question, this time to Jack.

"Plenty of fire, eh?"

"Plenty," agreed Jack. "Wild like these mountains when it storms. Do anything a man can do, and sometimes more. Her mother got burnt in a forest fire, so she's the boss, even over her old man, and he's tough enough to fill his pipe with pine needles. If she does get Brian she'll take the steam out of him. If you don't believe it, say a word agin Rosalie."

"I wouldn't risk it," Bony said. "That Bessie's made of wire rope."

A minute or so later, there grew against the stars the shape of a building unmarked by lights, and Jack proceeded direct to it and in through a wide and high doorway. After the entry of the last horse and the rearguard, heavy doors thudded shut.

A match scraped to flame and a pressure lamp plopped and burned to steady radiance revealing a man, tall and gaunt, with a thatch of iron grey hair and dark eyes in a rugged face. He held the lamp high to bring to reality the heated horses and their loads, Steve and Jack, and the girl Bessie. He said, with a slight brogue:

"No more troubles?"

"Nat, here, saw those men walking up and down Sandy Creek before sundown," replied Jack. "Still lookin'. I told you how Nat bluffed 'em, Tim."

"You did so," O'Grady advanced to hold the lamp closer to Bony. "Glad to meet you, Nat. We like a man with a fast mind. Trust Mike Conway to choose well."

"Yes, Dad, Mike didn't choose too bad, did he?"

Beside the man's face appeared the oval face of his daughter. Her large brown eyes balanced out the complexion ruined by sun and wind, and admitted to the balance, the mass of brown hair tied in a pony tail. Her eyes studied the new man, studied every feature of the brown face. She was wearing a short reefer coat, buttoned tightly, dungaree trousers and well worn, elastic sided boots.

"I'm glad I pass," Bony said, smilingly, his gaze moving

from her to O'Grady, and back again. "I apologise again for manhandling you."

"Ah, how was that?" asked O'Grady.

Bessie told about her reception at the night camp on the ledge, and O'Grady laughed quietly, and repeated his preference for a man who can think quickly. Then he broke into swift action.

"All right, bhoys. Down below with the merchandise."

He gave the lamp to Bessie and took a spade and cleared the floor covering of dry earth from a trap door, and Steve and Jack began unloading the packs. Bessie slipped down into the cellar and there lit another lamp, and when she came up and found Bony unslinging sack-protected liquor containers, she urged him to stop and sit with her on an empty case.

"They can manage," she said. "Talk to me. I want to know about you."

He related sketchily his assumed history, watching her very-much-alive face and eyes alternatively with the men lowering the containers down the cellar steps to O'Grady. She wanted to know how he had bluffed the bushwalkers with boulders and then she asked about Rosalie, and that he was to tell Rosalie how much she was looking forward to seeing her at the festival. It was now that Bony made his decision.

"You told me you'd do anything for her. True?"

"Of course. Did she . . . "

"She wants you to do something for her now." Two fingers touched his lips to warn her. "She has a boy friend in Sydney. She wants you to post a letter for her, secretly."

Nodding assent, she, too, watched Steve and Jack at work, and the letter slipped swiftly into her pocket.

"That will be okay, Nat. Tell her so." Her eyes were shining with excitement. "Did she say who he is? Is she happy, real and true?"

"No to your first question. I think yes to the second. How long is it since you saw her?"

"At Christmas it was. We were over there for Christmas night." The brown eyes narrowed with introspection. "I think I can guess. I remember now Rosalie was a little bit different. Yes, I think I know who it could be. There was a man staying over at the Conways. I heard about him, but she didn't say a word to me. They found him knocking bits off the rocks near their waterfall. He was a teacher or something."

"Did you hear his name?"

"Yes. It was Hillier, Eric Hillier." Bessie was smiling. "I wonder! Perhaps it was after he went away that Rosalie fell in love, and wasn't sure enough to tell me at Christmas. If you get the chance, Nat, you tell her my guess. Say I guess before I see who the letter's for." The stowing of the containers being completed, O'Grady was ascending the steps, and Bessie laughed and exclaimed: "What a trick, Nat! Those men didn't like those boulders falling on them, I bet."

She chatted and teased as the horses were loaded with bags of cattle cake, and finally Bony produced his delivery note and had O'Grady sign the receipt. He said then he had to sign for the back loading, and insisted when O'Grady and Jack both said that was not now necessary.

"Well, that finishes it," O'Grady announced. "You tell Mike and the others we'll be over at the festival. Tell Mate Conway we're looking forward to her pasties, and tell Red we hope he's got a lot of that special dandelion wine left."

"And tell Rosalie from me that I'm counting the days," added Bessie.

The lamps were extinguished and the doors opened to permit the smugglers to leave in the dark. The girl accompanied them to the gate from where the return track was known to Jack. She squeezed Bony's arm, and sent by Jack her 'love' to Brian Kelly, and as they departed Bony heard her closing the farm gate.

Right now Bony was pleased with himself. His ambushing sustained his vanity and fed a life-long spirit of rebellion against authority. He felt he was in the position of the trusted scientist being investigated by security. He felt like a spy being spied upon. It wasn't so, of course, but this was how the presence of other investigators into matters on which he was assigned now affected him. No man likes his ability to be questioned, his reputation to be disputed; therefore those alleged bushwalkers, or others of the police or the Customs Department opposed to him, were rather more than competitors.

This had been the underlying motive for his action of ambushing, preserving his territory against intruding strangers. However, he had, by so doing, strengthened his position with the men of Cork Valley and further strengthened it by the assumed indignation of the carelessness of leaving horse tracks, and the temerity which dictated the back loading of cattle-feed instead of sugar for the distillation of Mountain Dew.

He had reported seeing those bushwalkers late the previous afternoon, when they were probably miles from the valley of shallow streams, intending to add to his fellows' difficulties and gain not a little by surmounting them himself. All this contributed to the satisfaction he now felt. Having been assigned to investigate homicide, homicide would be entirely his concern, and smuggling merely a step or two towards finding the murderer of Eric Torby.

It was perhaps the dark night, the rough going, the spice of adventure which controlled Bony this night. Had it been broad daylight, and his associates policemen, the reactions of Inspector Bonaparte might have been very different.

Anyway, he liked the men of Cork Valley. They were a kindly lot. Moreover, as himself, they were born natural rebels. An Australian Prime Minister once said: "You can do anything you like as long as its legal." So you can raise your own salary and increase the perks, if you make it legal. Legality is King; Morality is like 'Monopoly', a game for a quiet evening.

Some time about midnight Brian Kelly and his dogs appeared to report all quiet ahead. They off-loaded and fed the horses, made a fire and camped until daylight, and when Bony awoke he found himself amid great boulders lying under the vast balcony of bulging rock at the foot of a mountain.

They were in a narrow gorge, and water music played to the new day. He took towel and soap to the racing stream, and was captivated by the beauty of the towering walls of grey and brown 'bricks' of which they were built. The air was crisp and distance was dwarfed, and on the narrow grass banks of the stream rabbits fed and two deer grazed. The deer fled when he approached, but the rabbits merely ambled a short distance away and regarded him with mild curiosity.

Jack was the next man to ease himself from his blankets. He proceeded to halter the horses and, with three on each side, led them from among the boulders to the stream where he found Bony madly splashing about and entirely naked.

"You gone wonky?" he asked with spurious nonchalance.

"Not yet, but I will if I can't scoop out some fish for breakfast," replied Bony. "Enough fish in this stream to feed Cork Valley. Stand back. Here's some more. They're half-pounders at least."

"You keep going, Nat," Jack encouraged him, and took the horses down stream. Brian appeared; when he saw two fish flapping on the grass, he ran up stream and flung off his clothes, then splashed and beat the water down towards Bony.

The fish were bled and grilled on the hot coals while the horses munched chaff and the tethered dogs fed on scraps. It was a wonderful morning, and physically, Bony felt right on top. Steve vented his peculiar rumbling laughter.

"Another crime to your record, Nat," he said, holding up the backbone of a three-quarter-pound trout. "Stealin' fish without a licence. Ten days in quod for fishing without paying the tax. You're lucky, though. 'deed you are. Next year we all get taxed for stealing the air into our lungs. Air and what you do in bed is the only two things left to be taxed."

Bony gazed at the three weathered faces of these scoundrels. He glanced at the opposite mountain wall, and knew he was no longer a stranger in this land of precipitous slopes and gushing streams, to men who had the courage to defy a bureaucratic State.

CHAPTER 16

Red Kelly Entertains

THE HOUSE had stood for a hundred and eleven years. Seen from Bony's potato field it was magnificent; viewed at close quarters it revealed all the years it had stared out over Cork Valley. Unhandsome, cold, vain and aloof, it seemed to enshrine the bitterness of an ancient race without a trace of that people's laughter to give it colour and warmth.

The great open porch-like entrance probably once had the protection of iron-studded doors, but now the flagged floor bore evidence of being used by poultry and hounds, and the hooks imbedded in the massive stone walls were probably used to tether horses while the master and his hunting guests ate lunch. A door opened inward from the rear wall of the lobby, and this late afternoon Red Kelly led a party of nine men into the great medieval hall of his house.

"Hey, there, Mary," he shouted, and his voice appeared to float away and hide behind the hanging tapestries, under the great armchairs, beneath the vast central table, large enough to dine a king and his entourage. He was wearing a suit of brown corduroy, and to Bony he fitted wonderfully into this huge background which made Lilliputians of ordinary men. Here, even Brian Kelly was dwarfed.

A woman appeared, large and stout, wearing a white apron over a black dress. She brought a tray loaded with decanters and glasses, and she set her cargo of cut glass on the table. Her expression was wooden, and softened only once when she looked at Brian Kelly. Red's guests were bidden to be seated.

Other than Bony and Brian, Jack and Steve, there were Mike Conway and Joe, again wearing his voluminous game-keeper's coat, and three men, strangers to Bony. The guests were told to serve themselves, and Bony found himself sipping first-class whisky. Habit was strong, and he proceeded to roll his unique cigarettes and make a little pile of them before lighting the first one.

"There was trouble," stated Red Kelly.

"We took all the ordinary precautions," stated Brian, and his father said, glaring at his son:

"Quiet, me bhoy. Jack, you tell of it."

In his imperturbable manner, the rotund man related the incidents of the trip, keeping everything in correct time sequence. He told how Bony had frustrated the bushwalkers; Bony had seen them late the next day at about the same place; the decision to bring back fodder to deliver to Moran, a farmer on the outskirts of Markham, instead of bringing sugar for Cork Valley. On the return, nothing had been seen of the bushwalkers and the decision to take fodder to Moran had been the cause of the delay in reaching Cork Valley again.

When he had finished no one spoke for a full minute, all apparently waiting for Red Kelly to make the next observation. He said:

"Bit o' bad luck."

No one offered comment on that. Mike looked across the table at Bony. His expression was vacant, but his dark eyes invited Bony to speak. Bony did.

"That's what Ned Kelly said before they hanged him."

Red Kelly's small blue eyes blazed with anger. His great hands bunched into rock-like fists, and his body crouched as though to spring over the table. He shouted:

"Ned said no such thing."

"If he didn't, he must have thought it," Bony said with unaffected calm. "The mistake Ned Kelly made at Glenrowan was the mistake you made by sending us on the track you did. Ned Kelly's mistake was to take the police too cheaply. That was your mistake. I don't understand why the police didn't catch up with you years ago."

"There are reasons," roared Red, standing the better to bring his fists down on the table which met the impact like a slab of granite. "You're a stranger here. You're a new chum. You know nothing. You're nothing but . . ."

"Break it up, Red," Conway said when the huge man stopped for breath. "There's no damage done, and we can learn I hope, to profit by mistakes."

"We can an' all," agreed Red at the top of his voice. "But it's me as tells you we made no mistake by taking that road. It lies with young Brian. He should have know'd the train was being followed."

"I did know, and when I did, I sent word to Jack and the others. So what are you yelping about?"

"And now 'tis me own flesh and blood that's cheeking me. By the living——"

Red pushed back his chair to topple with a crash on the tiled floor. Brian stood and backed away from the table, and there they glared like a couple of dogs who had been in many a fight with neither gaining the upper hand. Jack and Steve continued stoically to smoke and lower the tide-in-glass. Mike Conway regarded his hands lying idly on the table, and Bony stubbed out a cigarette and lit another. No one spoke until the Kellys sat down.

"Now perhaps Mister Nat Bonnay, ye'll be kind enough to oblige with your quare views," sneered Red.

"Someone told me that this Cork Valley back-door trading has been going on for a hundred years," began Bony, and was stopped by Red who wanted to know who told that lie. Softly and distinctly, Bony said: "Shut up! How the devil do I know who told me? Think I'm a tape recorder? A hundred years ago, fifty years ago, even ten years ago, there weren't the people in Australia there are today.

"We found trout in one of the streams, and where there's fish in these mountains, there could be anglers to catch them. Years pass. Times change. If those bushwalkers hadn't got on to our tracks this trip, then other people might do so on the next trip or the one after. So, from now on we'll have to have a scout behind us as well as ahead."

"That's not tellin' us anything," shouted Red.

"True," agreed Bony. "There's something else I won't be telling you, and that is when a pack train leaves a trail deep enough for a blind man to follow with the point of his stick,

It's just childish. Now pipe down. You can roar and yell in a minute. If there is no way over the mountains without leaving horse tracks on soft ground, then something should be done with the horses' hooves, for no one can give them wings.

"If you have to take a string of horses across soft country; if you have to make the trip before the winter weather is well set in, when it's cold and bleak and wet enough to keep strangers at their television sets at home; if you have to go on thinking there can't be strangers in the mountains because there were no strangers a hundred years ago, then you'll have to ask Nat Bonnay how to carry on back-door trading without getting yourselves jugged. That is telling you something, Red."

The big Irishman's red hair seemed to stand up from his head, and his beard to stand out from his face. Splashing whisky into a glass he drank it like water to wash down a pill. His breathing rasped through his nostrils as he fought hard to maintain a degree of control which for him was an achievement.

"Tell us something," quietly invited Mike Conway, stressing the pronoun.

"I once worked camels on stony country," Bony said. "As you know, they have rubbery soles which are tough enough on sandy ground but may be cut and split on sharp stones. For those camels, we made leather boots. They saved the camels' feet, and they wore well. A feller got the idea of robbing a small-town store. He made leather boots for his horse, and to the soles he tacked ordinary iron horseshoes back to front. The horse couldn't gallop in the shoes, but that didn't much matter as the robber had plenty of time. Anyway, when the policeman, and the locals with him, found themselves astray, the feller was well home with mum and the kids. Just an example of what can be done."

"Ned Kelly invented that idea back in year one," argued Red Kelly.

"Lot to it," said Steve, and Jack nodded sagely. "Soft leather shoes, made on the floppy side, would stop anyone knowing if we was going or coming. The tops could be laced above the hocks, and put on or taken off in a jiffy."

"Wouldn't bluff anyone," grumbled Red.

"Bluff most people anyway for an hour or two to give us time to get away," Jack said, and Brian nodded agreement, perhaps merely to disagree with his father. "We could go the whole hog and make leather shoes with the horseshoes back to front, like that store robber. Good for you, Nat. Any more bright ideas?"

"Yes, but I'll keep 'em in the box till wanted. Mightn't need the shoes. There must be ways of going through the mountains without leaving tracks. Let me prospect, and I'll find ways." Bony gambled. "I'll bet anyone and all of you that I could take the horses to O'Grady and bring back the sugar, all on my ownsome. And start tonight."

"Be damned if I don't think you could," shouted Red. "I'm alterin' me opinions of you, Nat, me bhoy. 'Tis an idea I've had for some toime, about leather shoes for the horses, but I clane forgot about it till you mentioned it just now. An' you'll be going for the sugar tonight."

"Not tonight."

The clear and soft voice directed all eyes to Mike Conway, abashed Red Kelly into astonishment, caused Joe to look up from studying his fingers. The words were barely important. It was the underlying strength of will revealed by the tones as well as the enunciation.

"You fellows were right not to bring back sugar. We aren't that short of it. There was a risk, and we don't operate with a risk. As for taking that particular track to O'Grady's place, there was nothing wrong with that decision. How those fellows sneaked in behind the train, we don't know. It could have been accidental, not intentional. We aren't sure who they are. Nat will not take on the trip to bring back sugar, just to prove he can do it without being questioned. We shall not make further trips until we can be sure, or as sure as possible, there are no risks."

"But. . . . But . . ." exploded Red, and Mike cut him off.

"We are not completely dependent on our back-door

trade," Conway continued, as though addressing a theological class. "Prosperity or starvation isn't determined by it, as once it was. As Nat pointed out, times have changed. However, we haven't changed. We are still agin the gov'ment, and to be agin the gov'ment is a good thing, keeping alive in us the spirit of independence and the will never to be subservient to political or bureaucratic pressures. Therefore, we carry on our back-door trading by taking every precaution to avoid blaming disaster on bad luck."

One of the strangers nodded his head like a mechanical toy. He drank and his deep upper lip lifted in disdain. Jack nodded with swifter approval of what Mike had said and Brian appeared to be waiting for something expected. Red Kelly emitted a sound akin to a board being wrenched from the floor and tossed whisky down his throat as if to smother another imaginary pill. With vast contempt, he shouted:

"Scotch! Bliddy muck! The Scotchmen never made dinkum whisky after the English conquered 'em." He rolled away to a wall, lifted a corner of the tapestry, kicked a stone at the base of the wall, when a section swung outward to reveal an enormous cupboard. From the cupboard he snatched a two-gallon demijohn, slammed the stone door shut, and returned to the table. "Let's have a man's snort. Pour that canine's water on the floor, Joe." He flicked the demijohn to a shoulder with one hand, drew the cork with the other and filled several glasses with the pristine Mountain Dew. Conway, evincing disapproval, said:

"You were closest to those bushwalkers, Nat. D'you think they are the same pair who came down into the valley that day?"

"I wasn't close enough to be sure, Mike. They were the same build. Give me a week, and I'll prove it one way or the other."

"How?" barked Red.

"Tracking them down."

"You do think a lot of yourself," sneered Kelly.

"I try to offer helpful suggestions," Bony again needled. "I don't run my head against a rock to tell how soft the rock is. I go tracking those strangers, and I run the risk of being recognised by them, and have the police after me. Not much of a risk, but I would take it rather than let a couple of wandering spies stop me in a bit of trading under the lap. This experience we had might make you all polish your brains. If you had had a taste of gaol like me, they'd be polished right now. Like to know what's wrong with you?"

Red flexed his mighty arms. His beard stood out and his eyes became pinheads of blue. He could have been comical were it not for the menace oozing from him.

"Quiet, Nat," said Mike. But Bony kept testing the Ned Kelly angle.

"You've been living too close. You've lost touch with the outside world. You think the police are like those that Ned Kelly made dance all those years ago. I've read about Ned. He did have brains, and he kept 'em polished until he lost out at Glenrowan. By that time he was too confident in himself and too contemptuous of the dopes in uniform who were chasing him. And so he took unnecessary risks, had a gay time with the people at the hotel, and was cornered."

"I'll have nothing agin Ned Kelly," roared Red. "I'll . . ."

"Ned Kelly had it in him to conquer Australia," continued Bony. "He could have been King of Australia, but the crown was too heavy for him to lift off the ground. He shouldn't have got himself muddled with booze. He should have kept his brain clear to keep on thinking with. Like you, Red. Just like you. Only you never had a brain to think with. So shut up and sit down."

Red swept back his chair. He waved his arms. He expanded his chest, and made the same mistake he had made at the granite wall. He rushed Bony. He was lifted to the ceiling, appeared to twist there, and crashed on his back. Bony sensed the others were standing behind him, and he whirled to meet the attack. Finding them still passive, he waited again for Red, and Red staggered to his feet, pressed both hands to the back of his head and shouted a torrent of threats.

"I'll mangle you, ye black bastid. I'll beat you to a pulp like they done Kelso. By the living. . . ." The others were now shouting to stop him. Conway stood on the table, a glass in one hand, a full decanter of whisky in the other. Red swayed and went on and on, much of it making no sense. He began to circle Bony, as though they were two gladiators. His back was eventually turned to Conway, and Mike stepped down from the table to a chair, from the chair to the floor, and applied the decanter to Red's head at the place where the floor had hit it.

Slowly Red Kelly turned about. With dimming eyes he saw Mike with the decanter. His shouting stopped, and he laughed. His knees sagged and he slumped into his son's arms. Mike said, calmly:

"No time for fighting. Let's have a drink."

Brian laid his father out, stood up, grinned and said:

"Nice work."

Bony shook his head as though he had been stunned with the decanter, shrugged despairingly at his failure to understand these Irishmen, and poured a half tot for himself.

CHAPTER 17

An Important Affair

GRANDMA CONWAY gazed into the heart of the fire. Her dark eyes were introspective, and the expression on her face was saint-like. Only her hands, white and fragile, indicated her thoughts when the fingers of one caressed the fingers of the other. She was oblivious of Mate Conway working over her stove, and of Rosalie who was setting the table, for she was seeing pictures of the great room in Red Kelly's mansion.

She had been married in that room nearly seventy years ago. She had been there at a dozen wakes. She knew the history of every tapestry, every painting of the Kellys', the hearth where the end of a tree trunk burnt, the trunk that someone would now and then 'nudge' in from outside the house with a crowbar. That room, that great house, was the pride of all the Kellys, and all the Conways, and all the latecomers who had married into the two families. Abruptly the house, the room, the familiar things attached to the years of her life were banished by a voice saying with execrable imitation of the Irish brogue:

"I've been after thinkin' of ye these last two days, Grandma. An' I'm hoping now all is well with ye."

Her dark eyes stared into the bright blue eyes, to examine the newly-shaved face and the sleek black hair brushed straight off the broad forehead.

" 'Tis a pity you don't think more about me, Nat, and then ye wouldn't be fightin' Red Kelly over there in his own house."

"There was no fight, Grandma. Besides, Red likes fighting, and a guest owes it to his host to oblige him in every way. Do you remember the time you saw him rise up in the air above the wall?"

"I do, indeed."

"Well, this afternoon it was the ceiling that stopped him." The straight line of her mouth melted into a curve at each end. "Just a little trick, you know. Feller gains speed with his legs, lifting himself along. He steps into another feller's cupped hands, and the hands are raised, and up he goes like the cow that flew over the moon. That's not fightin', is it now?"

"I've been told all about it, Nat," Grandma said, trying really hard to straighten the line of her mouth. "What made it bad was that you damaged his ceiling."

"Oh, now, now! I didn't touch his ceiling. When Red got up there he put his boot through it. I wasn't anywhere near him."

"Quite right. About ten feet under him," supported Mike. "Besides, Grandma, Nat promised to go over some time and help Red to plaster up the hole."

The old lady's eyes flashed. She said:

"I didn't know about that. You never told me."

"Then I must have forgotten in the excitement of telling you about the fight. When Red came out of retirement, Nat was sitting on his heels beside him. First thing Red saw was a glass of whisky. Then he saw Nat, and began to get angry again. Nat said: 'Have a snort. Stop you being giddy.' Red said he wasn't giddy. He took the glass and emptied it. He smashed it on the floor, and held it by the bottom to use the splintered part to go for Nat. Then what!"

"The devil! What?" Grandma breathed, looking at Bony to be sure his face wasn't cut to ribbons.

"Nat said: 'As one dinkum Irishman to another, why not call it a day? After all, this is your house, your whisky, and your ceiling,' Red said: 'What ceiling?' and he looked up and saw the hole. He was sitting on the floor, mind you. He tossed the broken glass aside, and looked up. Then he looked at Nat, and Nat was smiling. Then he roared with laughter, and Nat offered to help him plaster it. And that's the way it ended."

"All nice and friendly," added Bony. "Red has his good points."

"And what was that about Kelso?" asked Grandma, shrewdly watching him.

"Kelso!" Bony echoed. "Oh, he said something about doing me over like Kelso, or it might have been hell-so. Red was so worked up he couldn't get the words out properly. Anyway, he was in good humour when we left him. The ceiling can be repaired with a step ladder and ten pounds of plaster of Paris. Told him I'd pay for it, but he wouldn't listen."

"Why should he?" Grandma's eyes were opal red as they reflected the firelight. "Nat, will ye do something for me?"

"What a thing to be after askin' me," he cried, again with the dreadful brogue. "Tell it quick."

She refused to surrender to his raillery, and it was clear that Mike, too, thought the moment serious. She said:

"Will ye promise never again to stir Red up? He's a good friend and a bad enemy. We don't want enemies in Cork Valley ever again. Promise, Nat, my bhoy, promise."

"Of course, Grandma. I wasn't thinking about the valley in general. You know, Red needles me, so I needled him in return. Didn't think. Yes, I'll be glad to promise that. Promise you anything."

"I believe you would," the old woman said happily, and then could restrain her laughter no longer. "Say, Nat, how big is the hole in his ceiling?"

"Couple of feet long by a foot wide, not counting the cracks."

"Put half his leg through it as well as his boot," Mike said, joining in his grandparent's mirth. "I thought to see him go up altogether, and out through the roof. Oh, Nat, that's a trick and a half."

"And the next trick's on the table getting cold," interrupted his wife.

Seated at his accustomed place with Joe on his right and Rosalie on his left, Bony wondered at himself being so happy among these people. For long periods he had found it so easy to forget why he was here. He was actually enjoying this sojourn among them. He had enjoyed every moment of the trip to O'Grady's farm, and the smuggling of illicit liquor troubled him not at all. It was only at odd moments—when the matriarch watched him for the effect the name Kelso might have on him, for example—that he was reminded of a dead man whose demise he was here to investigate.

Hard to remember he was a detective-inspector! Of course it was. There was Joe even now winking with ill-suppressed humour over the recent brawl with Red Kelly. There was dark and flashing Rosalie, giving him covert glances betraying her anxiety to hear if he had 'posted' her letter.

The girl would be his immediate problem, and he would have to give thought to its solution. If handled properly he might gain much, and there again he was off at a tangent. He would have to tell her that Torby was dead, and he would have to use her grief to forward his investigation, tax her loyalty, perhaps, even to her own people. Thinking they might remark on his being too reserved, he said to Joe:

"What is this Cork Valley Festival I've been hearing about?"

The red-headed boy grinned and was about to answer for Joe, when he was prevented by Mike Conway. It was surprising how often that quietly spoken, unobtrusive man revealed a forcefulness of character only at moments of his own choosing. There was no ruggedness about him, any more than in his speech. When stepping down from the table and wielding the decanter he had shown the aloof detachment of a scientist terminating an experiment.

"Our festival is something of a secret, Nat," he said. "I hope no one tells you of its precise nature so that you will be pleasantly captivated by the spirit of it. What year was it first held, Tony?"

The red-headed boy answered promptly:

"Eighteen eighty-one." The boy was delighted by the request, regarding Mike with open affection. No one feared Conway, no one of his own family.

"And the day and the month?" pressed Mike.

"The eleventh day of November," was the prompt answer.

Now Mike was smiling, and although the length of the table separated them, Bony could detect the smile in the dark, intelligent eyes.

"Well, Nat, there is the original date," Mike went on. You went to a good school, and I'm sure you didn't waste your time there. Our festival is the oldest in Australia. It is unique because it isn't held to attract tourists, it isn't associated with the raising of money, and it is genuinely democratic in character. You may guess the motif."

"All right, I'll try," responded Bony, laughingly. "Now it can't be a festival of flowers like the Bowral show, or a festival of pineapples, or a tuna festival, because . . . wait a moment. When is this festival of yours to be held?"

"July the first," he was told.

"Then it cannot be a festival of flowers, a pea festival, a tuna festival, because the season isn't right. Is it a potato festival?"

"No," replied Mike, and chuckled at a joke appreciated only by himself.

Bony smiled at young Tony, and at several other children, all waiting with thrilled expectancy.

"Melon Festival? Snowball Festival? Ah! Is it a Wine Festival?"

Joe Flanagan broke into loud laughter. Mike tossed his head and smiled broadly. Old Mrs Conway laughed, and the children shrieked. One of them said Bony must keep guessing, and Grandma whispered hastily to Mike and his wife. Mike agreed, and said to Bony:

"Anyway, Nat, while you're thinking out more guesses, and you will be told when you guess right, what d'you say to giving some gum-leaf music at the festival? We have an accordian band and you could play in it, too. You could render a solo item now and then."

"I'd be glad to," assented Bony. "But wait a moment. I know very few tunes; in fact only 'Tipperary' and 'Danny Boy'. I've had no real practice for years. And besides, I suppose at the festival mostly Irish airs will be played."

Mike nodded agreement, and the old lady again hurriedly whispered.

"There's time to practise, Nat. Rosalie could play the Irish tunes for you to learn."

Now all eyes were directed to the girl who sat straight and smiled. Quickly she nodded, and Bony fancied he detected eagerness in the depths of her large and expressive eyes. He said:

"Well, why not! If Rosalie will be patient with me. I mightn't learn fast, but I'm a trier."

"They could practise on the old piano in the next room," Mate Conway suggested, and was opposed by Rosalie.

"That instrument hasn't been tuned for years. I couldn't bear to play on it. The one at school is all right. Nat could come there after school."

There was the hint of time spent on consideration, so Bony caught time by the throat.

"All right, then. Thanks Rosalie. I'll be there tomorrow when school comes out, and you can change over from arithmetic to music. I'll gather some of my special leaves, and if we don't raise the roof at the festival, I'm not Nat Bonnay. D'you know 'When Irish Eyes are Smiling'? Can you play the 'Irish Washerwoman'?"

Rosalie nodded, and her eyes were bright with unwonted enthusiasm, causing Bony inwardly to shrink from the thought of her being hurt. Then ideas were discussed in general, and Bony learned there would probably be six or seven accordions, and half a dozen fiddles, and old Pat Mulvaney would be bound to come with his warpipes. Joe Flanagan assured him it would be a good shivoo, and Bony was sure it would be with a band numbering all those instruments.

The dinner ended and the children withdrew, and after the usual cup of wine had been imbibed, Mike Conway invited Bony to 'talk awhile' in his office. Sitting sideways at his roll-top desk, with Bony relaxed in a second chair, he opened with:

"I'm glad you promised Grandma not to rouse Red up any more. He's always been a difficult customer. As you so aptly put it, he's got nothing to think with. He went to college like the rest of us, but they wouldn't have him there long because of his temper and because they couldn't knock any sense into him. So for peace's sake, go easy on him, will you?"

"Certainly," Bony instantly agreed. "What happened this afternoon was my fault, but . . ."

"I know. He's the most irritating Irishman ever whelped. Given us a lot of trouble from time to time, but as I've told you he's one branch of a family and we're another. We all have to stick together or all fall apart. There's something else." The dark eyes were hard, the pupils almost an unrelieved slate. "Steve told me about the pistol young Brian carried, and how you made him give it up, and disposed of it. You did a good job, Nat, and we're grateful. Grateful, too, that you didn't mention it when telling Red off."

"Enough fuel on the fire, Mike. Yes, I couldn't stand for carrying a pistol. Trouble started would mean trouble mountain high. No real intention of using it, but you never know."

"No, you never know. Anyway, young Brian will be going abroad in a few weeks, and I'm beginning to feel I shall be easy in mind when you take over the scouting. In spite of what I said about not being dependent on the trade, the trade is valuable. Keeps us a lot of contacts outside. We don't send raw stuff out, only properly matured stuff, as you can judge for yourself. No jungle-juice about the Cork Valley product. Family secret handed down for generations. You have any private thoughts on those bushwalkers?"

Bony nodded thoughtfully, and took time before replying:

"Could be police. Could be excise men. They were excise men who nailed a couple of fellers with a still out from Tenterfield a few years ago."

"We've had them down here, too, in the past years. What I don't understand is why those two are operating just now. We haven't been trading since last August. Never do in the summer. Now, on our first trip this winter, they are poking about."

"Well, why let it worry you?" Bony asked blandly. "Two among these mountains are like a couple of bull ants on a stick floating down a flooded creek. You want to swim the creek, you don't play with the stick when crossing. The next time you send a pack train to O'Grady, let me do the scouting.

And not immediately in front of the train, but two days before it starts."

The dark Irish eyes studied Bony's face, feature by feature, and the dark hair glinted in the light when Mike nodded his agreement.

"Another thing, Mike, I ought to be out keeping an eye on those bushwalkers. I'd find what they are after, and who they are, and when the mountains were clear of them."

For a long minute, Mike Conway gazed at a point beyond Bony.

"I'll think about it, Nat. Anyway, there'll be no more trips until after the festival." He smiled. "That is a very important affair, Nat."

CHAPTER 18

The Musicians

THE MAIN result of the smuggling trip to Timothy O'Grady was that Bony received the freedom of Cork Valley, and, wisely, he did not endanger it by a rash word or an impatient action. While a colleague would have been anxious about his wife and family, or perturbed that his superiors would expect him to have the assignment completed and nicely wrapped up within the proverbial five minutes, Bony was confident of his wife's understanding of his long absences, and scornful of the opinions, expectations or desires of any superior. He would conduct the inquiry in his own manner. What people sitting behind desks happen to think wasn't the smallest consequence, except when they interfered, and Bony was quick to resent this.

He would like to have investigated those bushwalkers, and had they proved to be policemen or other officials, he would have led them a dance they would have remembered for a long time. However, in view of Mike Conway's persistent refusal to grant this permission, he was happy to accept it and wait for the mountain to come to Mahomet.

He was not now expected to return immediately after dinner to his room under the shed. Old Mrs Conway liked to detain him for a few minutes, and, the night following the return from the trip, Joe Flanagan invited him to a friend's house to watch television. Perhaps for Joe, as well as Bony, the advent of television was a boon to mankind, since it prevented idle gossip.

Back at his digging, Bony spent the following days beneficially exercising both his body and his mind. He was entertained again by the kookaburras and the wren, and he had several visitors. One morning Red Kelly rode over to tell him that he had repaired the ceiling, adding: "To hell with you, Nat, me bhoy. How do you do it?" Joe Flanagan came along one afternoon, hunting up hares, and he was joined by Jack from the big house who brought some stiff paper and a pair of shears. He asked Bony to cut a pattern for boots for horses.

Then there was the visit by Rosalie, accompanied by the schoolchildren who carried digging trowels, spirit jars, and a collection of boxes. It was a fine and warm afternoon, and she explained to Bony that they were all on a botany lesson. The elder boys were interested in the things that crept and crawled under the large stones which had fallen from the walls years ago, and the girls gathered specimens of plants which Rosalie named for them. No one was at all interested in the kookaburras, one of which now ran the risk of being speared by the fork as Bony worked.

The inevitable question was put to him when all the children were busy. Rosalie was aware of Grandma Conway and her spy glass, so she stood in an attitude of idle curiosity, watching the tubers being brought into the light of day.

"Did you pass on my letter, Nat?"

"I managed to give it to Bessie as you asked me to," Bony replied, not straightening his body, keeping his head low. "I hope it will turn out all right. Not against the Conways, that is. Bessie O'Grady said she'd do anything for you. Said for me to give you her love and hopes to see you at the festival."

"Thank you, Nat. When are you coming for the music lessons?"

"Whenever it suits you, of course. We should begin soon."

She went off with the children and then, within half an hour, as they were about to pass him on the way back, she suggested the school at five o'clock, and he agreed. Now and then he looked down at the party as it moved slowly beside the old wall to the river, and he hoped that his impulsive decision would not lead to disaster. The death of Hillier, or Torby, would inevitably hurt Rosalie Ryan, but it had to be accepted, and the hurt might be lessened by gentleness and sympathy.

At ten minutes to five he found Rosalie in the schoolhouse correcting papers. The school was conducted in a single classroom of the cream-painted building set upon its area of asphalt playing ground, dominated by the tall white flag mast.

"Oh, there you are, Nat! Are you ready?"

"Yes. I've brought my gum leaves, and I'm glad the children haven't stayed behind to hear us. It could be pretty weak at first."

Seated on a stool beside her at the piano, an expensive semi-grand, they faced across the room to the only doorway. There was a large window on the left-hand side; it had no blind and was shut. Beyond it across the playground were the settlement houses, and the sun was pouring the last of its rays across the room to the door which Bony had been careful to close. Privacy was assured until the interior lights were switched on, when anyone outside could see the musicians.

Rosalie began to play and he watched her fingers and admired her hands. She wore three rings, each a setting for an opal which he, knowing something of opals, valued at not less than a hundred pounds. His gaze moved from them to her wrists, to the white cuffs of her blue dress, which made it look a little like a uniform, to her face in profile, and finally to her hair. She said, the school teacher in command:

"You are not playing."

"I was listening to you playing to me."

"Look at the music. I'll begin again. Are you sure the others didn't see you give the letter to Bessie O'Grady? Now, with your leaf, please."

Rosalie played 'Come Back to Erin' and Bony did his best to accompany her. His mind was not on the work. He was away across the mountains, on that tor where he had steamed open the envelope and read the letter. He was watching again the flames of the little fire consuming it, seeing the white words on the black paper: 'Dear Eric'. His right hand held a pencil to paper he had brought with him, and the pencil wrote: 'Superintendent Casement. I am angry because men are masquerading in and about Cork Valley as bushwalkers. It was agreed, no interference, no surveillance. Kindly issue instruction to have them withdrawn. I am progressing as always on my assignment. Warm personal regards. B.'

"That was terrible," said the music teacher. "We will try again."

"I was thinking of Bessie," he lied, and the wailing of the leaf was like the wind whispering to the Blarney Stone. The noise stopped long enough for him to add: "She said she'd made up her mind to marry Brian Kelly." 'Come back to Erin' continued. They conversed in this manner.

"I wouldn't let her," Rosalie said with conviction.

"I much doubt that you or anyone in the wide world would stop Bessie doing anything she made up her mind to do."

"Bravado, Nat. Bessie is like that, on the outside."

"When I gave her your letter she didn't have time to glance at the name and address. She told me to tell you she guessed who the letter was for. She did, too. You see, I knew."

"That his name is Hillier."

"Yes. Bessie said that an Eric Hillier stayed with the Conways for some time. She said he was a teacher, and that he was also a geologist. Someone told her about him. You didn't, and that made her think you came to like him after she visited here at Christmas."

"Bessie is very wide awake, Nat." Rosalie started to play 'My Wild Irish Rose' saying: "Now we will work hard, if you please."

For once in his career, Bony had to curb his questioning. This charming Irish girl was no love-lorn maiden ready to confess her thoughts and longings to any sympathetic listener, and apart from the sense of family loyalties, she was unusually self-dependent. As far as she was concerned, having gained his cooperation in delivering the letter to Bessie O'Grady was sufficient.

This was how she thought at that first music lesson. It required many such interludes from teaching children and digging spuds, before he could extract from her the story of Eric Torby alias Hillier. Eventually she came more than half way to meet him and he was able to retain his pose of the sympathetic listener.

Torby had appeared one afternoon in mid-December. Together with a man named O'Halloran and Mike Conway, he had passed the school while she was giving the children physical exercise. He had stopped in the roadway, raised his hat to her and called a cheery greeting to the children.

At dinner that night and subsequently, he had occupied the place now taken by Bony. He had been interested in the school, and his knowledge of the curriculum and the classifications supported his claim to be a teacher. He was spending the summer vacation, as on previous holidays, on a walking tour, the main objective being to further his geological studies.

The man O'Halloran had found him eastward of the waterfall, and he said he had entered the valley from that direction the previous day. Answering their questions as to how he had descended from the rim, he had said he was an experienced mountaineer, but he didn't need to call on his experience to assist him although the descent needed careful negotiation.

Mike Conway invited him to stay on a few days, and he had been given the 'spare room'—Bony's underground room. It appeared that Torby's liberty was in no way curtailed, for he had wandered about the settlement, had prospected the river as far as Kelly's house, and had visited the schoolhouse where Rosalie had been giving music lessons to a most promising pupil. On one of these visits he had seen among the books on the library shelf a volume of reminiscences written by some very early pioneers at the invitation of the governor of the time, and this volume he had borrowed to read in his room. In this book Rosalie had found his message.

Having been at the settlement six days, Torby departed without telling her he was returning to the city. He had been offered a lift as far as Wollongong. Mike told her at dinner that day, and the following day one of the children had returned the borrowed book to the school.

Rosalie admitted that she was piqued because Hillier hadn't said goodbye before he left. Two days before Christmas, at dinner, Mike Conway had produced and read a letter which he said was written by Hillier, thanking them all for their hospitality, and that the writer had given his address at some street in Rydalmere, Sydney. A few days after Christmas, Rosalie had written to him, hoping to begin a correspondence, and had received no reply.

Finding Hillier's note in the borrowed book gave Rosalie grounds for several surprises. Here he gave his address as No. 10 Evian Street, Rose Bay. Here he admitted warm regard for her, and his intention of coming back to Cork Valley. Now suspicion arose that Mate Conway had stopped her letter to Eric Hillier.

All this she admitted to Bony, admissions before he could begin his very careful cross-examination, and the following transpired over the course of several music lessons.

"Do you remember the date that Hillier returned to Wollongong?" he asked.

"Oh yes," Rosalie replied, as though to forget such a date was impossible. "It was December 20."

On December 21 the body of Eric Torby had been found on the road to Bowral.

"Would you allow me to read the message he wrote in the book?"

"I don't know, Nat," she answered hesitantly. "Yes, if you want to."

"You could let me borrow the book."

"I tore out the leaf. I keep it in my keep-sake box in my room."

Soundlessly, Bony sighed. He said: "It doesn't matter. When did you read it last? Every night, I suppose."

"No, it was several nights ago. I know every word by heart."

"You say that Mike told you all at dinner that Hillier took the opportunity of a lift to Wollongong. By who?"

"I couldn't say. I don't know."

"But it wasn't Mike Conway?" pressed Bony.

"I could not be sure about anything that day, Nat. You see, the day wasn't important until . . . until dinner that night. Why bother? Someone must have taken him to Wollongong. He wasn't here at lunch."

"No one appeared to be worried about him after he left?"

"It's funny you ask that," Rosalie said. "I had the feeling

that Mate was until Mike read Eric's letter at dinner, the letter thanking us all for being nice to him."

"And no one could have stopped your letter going out to Hillier in the post excepting Mate?"

"She always collects the mail from the box and puts it into the bag, and seals the bag. Anyone going to Bowral or Wollongong takes the bag there."

Later, choosing the moment carefully, Bony asked the girl: "Why would Mate stop your letter?"

"Because she wouldn't want me to fall in love with an outsider. Eric is, you know. He isn't even Irish. Besides . . ."

Her sentence was not completed until two evenings later, when Bony learned that the Conways hoped Rosalie would marry a Kelly. Returning to the subject, he reminded her that Brian appeared not to be favoured, and she said:

"When he came back from school, Grandma told me. I told them I'd never love Brian well enough to marry him, and they said, I mean Grandma said, love had nothing to do with marrying. Anyway, Brian's all right, but I had to smack his face one evening. I'll marry who I want to."

He learned that the man O'Halloran was of the Kelly side of the valley, and that the place where O'Halloran discovered Torby, or Hillier, was a quarter of a mile or less on the east side of the waterfall. He asked Rosalie if she had ever been to that particular place, and was told no one was permitted to go near the fall as the rock faces sometimes fell without warning.

The waterfall! He remembered vividly the coming of the car which had collected men and proceeded, without lights, in the direction of the waterfall.

CHAPTER 19

The Distillery

ALTHOUGH Bony's exploits on the trip across the mountains had gained him the freedom of Cork Valley, he had not yet uncovered any of the valley's secrets. After a long probation period, instinct told him that his movements were no longer questioned, but although he had been permitted to know that sugar is necessary in the production of 'dandelion wine', he had been given no hint of the locality of the production plant.

Having reached the decision to stick to the very last letter of his assignment, which meant finding the murderer of Eric Torby, and not concerning himself with Mountain Dew, or the payment of TV licences, he was brought back to the production of Mountain Dew because it probably triggered off Eric Torby's murder.

Bony was in no way concerned by the time it had taken him to find out that Torby had, indeed, been in Cork Valley immediately prior to the finding of his body. At least he had succeeded where a ponderous police investigation had failed, and it was pretty certain that if he had rushed hither and thither looking for illicit stills, he would not have progressed this far.

The two bushwalkers who had crossed the paddocks had been quickly apprehended and removed from the premises. Before them a disguised policeman had been taken out to the hospital. It now transpired that Torby had entered like a burglar and had been found the following day and brought to the settlement where, without doubt, he was meticulously watched.

Had Torby been sentenced to death and executed because he had learned the great secret of Cork Valley? If this were so the secret of Cork Valley was near the waterfall where

Torby's trail began, ending on a road many miles away.

Bony had not previously been given an assignment where the investigators had no prerogative to put direct questions. The girl had no actual knowledge of the manner of transport and the persons with whom Torby had departed from the settlement, and there was no other person he could question, nobody he could tackle with subterfuge without betraying an interest entirely divorced from his character of Nat Bonnay. Time was of no importance, however, and the unmasking of Torby's murderer was his only objective.

He could not be too openly persistent with his questioning of Rosalie. He could not strain her sense of loyalty to the point of being permanently rebuffed, and there were fifty questions left unasked which might well have clarified Torby's sojourn with the Conways.

Bony waited till midnight before leaving his underground room, wearing a dark blue working shirt in preference to the white one he usually wore in the evenings, and three pairs of socks instead of boots. There was a late moon shrouded by light fog; the night was not in total darkness.

He avoided the street, passing to the rear of the shed building, the houses and the school on that side, and he kept off the track taken by the car without lights. He had not left the settlement limits when a cold nose was pushed against his hand. It was one of the beagle dogs that had accompanied Brian Kelly.

"What do you want?" he asked softly, the thought occurring to him that the dog was scouting for Brian Kelly and would run off to inform on him. The dog stood still, his tail wagging, his stern unaffected. With his head slightly askew he regarded Bony with expressive and friendly eyes. "I think I know what you want. To go for a walk. Just bored doing nothing, eh?"

The beagle proved him right. The dog trotted sedately ahead.

Bony veered right to reach the track beyond the factory building, coming eventually to the piggery, betrayed by the smell and an occasional animal grunt, and for a moment or two he was unable to find a track proceeding from this place.

In daylight it would have been easy; as it was the dog saved him time.

The dog, once he had understood that the man's interest was not in pigs, made for a wall of low scrub and entered it. Bony found the scrub to be a narrow belt, and on the far side came to the twin impressions made by motor vehicles. A visitor to the piggery would not see this track proceeding from it.

Now, confident of the man's destination, the beagle trotted over the little-used track, its nose to ground, its rudder barely moving. On Bony's right was the river, and presently they came to a bridge which was little more than a wooden causeway. The bridge was ignored at the cost of wet feet. The little-used track missed the trees and seemed intent on keeping to grassy ground, and without doubt the man who drove the car without lights must have had super eyesight. Now and then the dog and the man were halted by a sound nearby of a rabbit, of a departing wombat or some other wild animal, but gradually the noise of the waterfall pervaded the night.

By day Bony had estimated the distance of the waterfall from the settlement as a mile. Now it seemed much farther. They came to the river again and another bridge, and this bridge, too, was ignored. The sound of the waterfall was all about them, and there emerged from the light fog the vertical curtain of lighter grey extending upward into the void. At the foot was a rugged natural catchment basin, into which the water fell with a ceaseless low roar, and at the outlets, which became the river, were several ram-pumps, doubtless servicing the settlement.

Beyond this basin the faint track did not proceed, and thus it might be presumed that the business of the motor driver was to inspect the pumps. According to Rosalie, it was to the eastward of this place that the man O'Halloran had found Eric Torby.

The dog was waiting patiently for Bony on the eastern side of the basin, and when Bony walked on, the beagle moved on at once, leading him through light scrub, and across broken. gouged, but dry watercourses. Abruptly the dog veered to the right, and as suddenly as he had come to the fall he now came to a wall of rock and realised he was hard against the mountain flank.

The beagle began to climb the rock face which was not truly perpendicular, then halted to look down when Bony hesitated to emulate this mountaineering feat. Being a dog and not a goat or a chamois, and unlikely to rock-climb for the idle fun of it, it was fairly obvious that the dog knew his job and was familiar with the way. He led Bony up into the void, like a fly on a wall with the light out.

It seemed to Bony that he and the dog ascended a thousand feet from the basin, both hemmed in by the noise of the fall and by the fog, when first one and then the other crawled over the lip of a ledge wide enough to take a car. No car, however, had ever been on this ledge.

Now Bony could smell smoke, the scent of burning gum-wood. He followed the dog, and presently came to what at first he thought was a tree trunk but which proved to be part of a hoist which, when thrust out from the ledge, would raise or lower heavy loads.

The ledge turned inward as Bony advanced, and the dark grey mistiness changed to bars of deeper grey. The rock became wet and threatened disaster to the unwary, and then Bony found himself in a corridor—rock wall on the left and sheeted water on the right. He was behind or inside the fall, and here was the opening to a cave.

Beside him stood the dog, for the first time disinclined to go on without him. On the floor of the cave was a hurricane lamp, and its light revealed a stack of wood and a dozen objects, including an array of pipes and a great cylindrical object which was plainly a water boiler. Steam was being emitted from valves, and at the foot the red glow of the fire escaped through the badly-fitted door of the firebox. Smoke and steam rose to the cave roof and created a dark cloud which came to the entrance and was wafted into the ceaseless curtain of falling water.

It was the perfect hideaway for an illicit still. And a still which had supplied the connoisseurs with mountain Dew for more than a hundred years! No one standing at the foot of the fall, or perched on the distant rim of the amphitheatre armed with a telescope would ever detect smoke and steam even on the brightest of days or a clear and frosty evening.

Keeping close to the rock wall, Bony moved into the cave. The dog declined to accompany him. Now Bony could see demijohns and glass jars on benches, steam boilers, a stack of potatoes and sugar sacks. In the irregular wall he found a niche, and here he remained and waited, for the lamp on the floor indicated the presence of at least one man.

It was well that Bony was cautious. Beside the big steam boiler appeared a man. He opened the front of the firebox and the glare revealed him to be Joe Flanagan. The ruddy light was reflected on his bald cranium as he tossed billets of wood into the furnace. Another man appeared, entering the cave from farther back, and the movement of his coat proved that inside the inner cave was an air fan. He was none other than Red Kelly.

"I'll be turning in, Joe," he shouted, quite unnecessarily, for in the main cave it was comparatively quiet. "Call me when you leave in the morning."

Flanagan slammed shut the furnace door, and said:

"I will that, Red. Want me tomorrow night?"

"No, we'll close down till after the festival. Tell Spade to come about noon to lend me a hand to store away."

Red Kelly disappeared into another cave, and within a few minutes reappeared wearing pyjamas. In the poor light he looked like King Kong prepared for the operating table.

"Remind Spade we'll want some grub," he shouted.

Joe said he wouldn't forget, and Red returned to the inner cave where presumably was his bed. Joe brought a sack which he folded on a case. He hung the lamp by a hook on a pipe, drew the case nearer the furnace, took from his voluminous coat a bottle, drank a shot of Dew, and then, having replaced the bottle, produced from the coat a hard-cover book. Then he sat on the case and prepared to relax.

From without came the muted noise of the fall competing with the inside sound of escaping steam, and for a few minutes

Bony pondered on his next move. He arrived at the conviction that further examination of this place might not be worth the risk of being discovered. Then the bell sounded.

It was so unexpected that it momentarily stunned Bony as it did Joe Flanagan. Joe dropped the book and stared at a point to his right. The bell stopped and the silence prodded Joe into movement. He snatched down the lamp and carried it to the right wall of the cave, where the light revealed a domestic indicator similar to the one in the Conway living-room.

"Hey, Red," he shouted, and Bony slipped away to the entrance of the cave and waited, peering round the bulge of rock. Kelly appeared. He must have heard the alarm for he asked no questions as he lumbered across the rock floor in his bare feet to stand with Joe.

"The first bridge," Joe observed, and there was now no amiability in his voice.

"Wait for the second," Red said, adding: "Could be a wombat like that time a year or more back. The second bridge will tell for sure."

Bony didn't wait for the second alarm, being unsure which of the two bridges were designated first or second and having to retreat swiftly to the cover of the bush on the floor of the valley. As he sped along the wide ledge he hoped he would find the place where the ascent from the valley had ended, for there was probably no other way down.

Then he saw the beagle. The dog was lying on the edge of the ledge, and he stood on seeing Bony, wagged his rudder, and disappeared, instantly ready to go ahead on the return 'walk'.

Bony slipped twice going down. Once he dislodged a piece of rock and heard it strike the rock base, and hoped the two men in the cave were still waiting for the second alarm.

With comforting level ground under him, and bush all about him, he waited for just one minute to see if Joe or Red would descend by that perilous pathway, and when neither appeared, he slipped further into the bush, and, with no thought of following the track, hastened as fast as the terrain and the night permitted back to the settlement.

Save in the living-room of Mike Conway's house, there were no lights in the houses, and Bony paused to peer around the edge of the side drapes.

He could see Mike and his wife standing before the bell indicator. Neither spoke nor turned away. They continued to stand regarding the indicator, and above their heads one white disc covered the black ground of the board. He was there several minutes, and both the Conways remained standing at the board, almost immobile in their intensity, until both moved as though released from the tension when the black orifice beside the white disc vanished as the second disc fell before it.

CHAPTER 20

Chief Tracker at Cork Valley

"Hi, Nat! Wake up!"

Bony groaned, turned on the bed, and again Mike Conway called him. He felt he could not have slept more than five minutes. He applied a match to the wick of his lamp, and when Conway came down the steps, with Red Kelly following, they saw a very sleepy Nat, now with his bare feet to the floor.

"Been some quare goings on, Nat, me bhoy," Red said, and sat on the only chair. "Thought perhaps ye might help us out."

Bony blinked his eyes, looked from Red to Mike, reached for papers and tobacco, and automatically fell to rolling one of his cigarettes.

"Funny time of night to have queer things going on," he said, faint complaint in his voice. "Helping out's all right but why not wait till daytime?"

"Well, 'tis like this . . ."

"I'll explain, Red," Mike cut in. "It isn't often we have intruders in this valley, Nat, but we seem to have had them tonight. They've been round the piggery, and they made their way out up by the road. We'd like to have you do some tracking first thing. You know, tell us how many there are, and all that."

Unhurriedly, Bony struck a match and lit the cigarette, both men watching him.

"That won't be hard," he said, blowing smoke. He glanced at the table clock, turning its face towards him. "Only five. Hour and a half to go to break of day. Why the rush? You don't expect me to track in the dark, do you?"

"True enough, Nat," agreed Mike. "Thought by the time you'd dressed and had breakfast, we'd be set to start. Besides, there are things to tell you, to explain so you'll understand."

"That's so, Mike," agreed Red. "Getting close to the festival, and we want the country clean for that. You'll co-operate, like?"

"Needn't ask. The coffee made yet?"

"That's the laddo," approved Red, standing, and Mike said he'd have the coffee brewed in two minutes and a drop of the 'doings' to help it down.

The fire was strong on the open hearth and the coffee was simmering on the stove when Bony arrived in the living-room. Red Kelly sat on a dining-chair, either nervous of occupying Grandma's wheeled chair or forbidden, and Mike served them with cups of coffee and cups of 'wine' which by now Bony had learned to appreciate and never to 'fumble'. The few steps from his shed to the house had informed him how cold the morning was.

"Well?" he said, interrogatively. "How d'you know you've had intruders? Lost any pigs or anything? And how do you know they've left by the road? Could be still in the valley."

"That's what we got to find out," rumbled the red giant. "Want you to track 'em if you can."

"How do you know you've had intruders?" persisted Bony.

"Because they were seen," replied Red.

"How many?"

"How do we know? That's what we want you to tell us."

"We're wasting time," quietly Mike interrupted.

"No, we're not. We're just getting down to rock, Mike."

It was peculiar that Conway seldom exerted himself in opposition to Red Kelly, intellectually so greatly inferior, until he despaired at the big man's stubbornness. His patience was extreme and yet limited; the patience of the doting parent of the unruly child. Now he said:

"They were not seen, Nat. They were heard crossing the bridges. Their weight on the bridges set off the alarm indicator. Mate and I watched the indicator up there tell the story. We were thinking that if you started from the top bridge as soon as day breaks you might catch 'em up."

"You're talking about the road we came in by that day

you picked me up, aren't you?" asked Bony, and Mike nodded. "Then having crossed the top bridge they would have to pass your brother's house. Didn't he happen to see them? He sleeps on the verandah. No dogs there?"

"He sleeps on the verandah, and he has a couple of dogs. They didn't pass the house."

"Then we'll find out which way they did go. Easy enough." Bony helped himself to coffee. "Have you had fellers mooching about the valley before I came here?"

"Well, now, that's sayin'," Red replied, now looking at Bony with dawning suspicion. "Now what . . ."

"The only count the police are on my tail for is thinking I stole a chook," Bony cut in. "The police aren't going to tramp all over these mountains and stalk around at night just to catch up with me, a chook thief. The reason isn't me. The reason must be something else, and that's nothing to do with me. Is this the first time you've had prowlers?"

"No," replied Mike. "We've had them in the past."

"Well, what did you do then?"

"Nothing—stayed quiet for a period."

"But we can't stay quiet for any period now," interjected Red. "There's the festival in ten days, and no one wants that put off."

"Why should it be?" asked Bony.

Red now looked at Mike, and Mike returned his look with pensive eyes. The question made both uneasy. Red began to explain, hesitated, left it to Mike, and Conway was less assured than Bony had ever found him.

"Our festival isn't public," he said. "Strangers aren't accepted. Us Conways and Kellys run it, and all our friends from outside come to it. Our neighbours, and suchlike. There's speeches, and games for the children, and a bit of play-acting at night, and as much food and drink, and the rest. We don't want to be spied on."

"Which is why we got to have the country all about nice and clean," added Red.

They saw Bony glance at the clock. They watched him make a cigarette, fingers automatically working, and even the huge Red Kelly conquered his impatience. It was the nearest approach either man came to suspecting this darkly inscrutable man was beyond the class of the ordinary country worker. Through the smoke he exhaled, Bony could see the danger in their eyes.

"Could be the same fellers we saw in the mountains, and they could be the same that crossed the valley when I was lifting spuds," he told them. "You'll recollect that after we got back from the mountain trip I wanted to go after those bush-walkers, and hang on their tracks for a month if necessary. You said, 'Oh, no, Nat. We couldn't trust you on that job. Why, you might join up with 'em and be a policeman.' "

" 'Twas no such thing," shouted Red, and Mike told him to keep his voice down."

"Near enough," agreed Bony, resuming his pose of in-dignant innocence. "You say the bridges are fitted with alarms. You say you heard those men passing over them on their way out. You don't say if you heard 'em come in, so they didn't come down here by the bridges. You say track them on out: I say back track 'em to find where they got in. Find out that, and that particular hole might be stopped."

"Now you're tarkin'," Red said, admiringly.

"Talking comes naturally," Bony claimed. "You have one-track minds. You send a scout on ahead, and haven't a scout behind. You want me to track ahead, and don't think to do some back tracking, like the aborigines would do. Now you run me up in the truck to the top bridge, and afterwards we'll back track from the piggery. Ever put the beagles to following a scent?"

"Them dogs are no good on anyone's smell."

"I'll make 'em good before I'm through," boasted Bony. "Let's go."

From the top bridge Bony tracked two men to the rim top, proved at several places with visual evidence that they had veered sharply away from the white house, and then bore back to gain the road taking them on to the Macquarie Pass. He described them as being heavier than Red, due to the packs they carried. He proved there were but two men, one of whom smoked 'tailor-made' cigarettes, and the other chewed gum, and both Mike Conway and Red were impressed. Bony was to learn that these men, and others of Cork Valley, were excellent bushmen: their sense of direction was almost instinctive, and they had a shrewd 'eye' for a level slope; but their knowledge of ground work was practically nil.

Following a late breakfast, the party went to the piggery where the ground was scored by the tracks of turning vehicles. The tracks of the two men were not here, but Bony found them at the first of the two bridges: the bridge they must have crossed when the alarm rang in the cave behind the waterfall, and he wondered just where they were when he was circling wide to get back to his underground room.

They had certainly crossed this bridge, for he found their tracks beyond it. He proceeded to back track. They had passed within a hundred yards of the base of the fall, coming from the east, from the point where, according to Rosalie, O'Halloran had found Torby with his geologist's hammer.

"You sure they came this way?" Mike asked.

"Clear enough to me," replied Bony.

"Didn't get closer to the fall?" added Red, looking at Bony with eyes almost buried by the deep frown.

"Not so far. We'll go on."

They hadn't gone on forty yards before Bony indicated footprints and outlined them for clarity. Further proof was discovered a few minutes later in the ashes of a small fire estimated to be not less than eighteen hours old.

"They could have camped here for a day," Bony estimated.

Red and Mike were told to remain at the ash heap, and they watched him circle the camp. On joining them, he said:

"They went to the fall where there's a sort of natural basin. Probably went for water because they came back here after lighting their fire."

"When? Can you say that?" demanded Red, and Bony said it was likely to be the previous evening. Red was relieved, and looked so. "Don't seem no use going any further."

"Must find out how they come down to the valley," objected Bony, and moved off before Red could argue.

The trail led them across deep water gutters, over grass patches and through low scrub to several stately ghost gums growing at the foot of a massive outcrop of granite streaked by pink quartz, and which formed the foot of cliffs rising to the rim. Here the trail turned left, parallel with the cliff front.

Abruptly, Bony halted and gazed at the granite outcrop. The others watched him, saying nothing. He advanced to the rock and bent to peer closely at it. Picking up rock fragments he examined them, and both men continued silently to watch.

He knew what he had found, but he made a pretence of being greatly interested in this place, before saying:

"Gold! Might be gold, but I wouldn't bet on it. You people been looking for it? Was gold ever found in the valley?"

"Me old father did a deal of prospectin' around, but he never come on to any," replied Red. "Faith, and I want a drink. What about going home for a toothfull?"

"An idea," Bony temporised. "Anyway, we might have got on to the purpose of those fellers being in the valley. They could be prospectors. Look! They broke bits off the rock here, and broke out pieces of the quartz. Only . . ."

"Only what?" insisted Red Kelly.

"Only they didn't do it yesterday. It was done weeks ago."

Red wanted the information to be more exact, and Bony evaded a closer estimate.

"Let's go on. Might find something else to tell a story."

"To hell with it, Nat, I'm needing a drink. It's nearly noon," protested Red.

Bony ignored the plea, and they were forced to follow him. The tracks led along the cliff base and skirted a section of almost sheer slope studded with protruding boulders and sparse trees, and where this section ended at another outcrop, Bony stopped and looked up to the summit from which a narrow ledge offered a foothold to a less precipitous slope.

"They came down here," he said and sat on a boulder to roll a cigarette.

Red and Mike Conway were regarding each other, Mike

with perplexity, and Red with his right eyebrow raised in what might have been humour had it not been for the light in his ice-blue eyes. Mike said, faintly defiantly:

"All right, we could have made a mistake."

"Yes, me for agreein'," Red said, coldly and quietly for him. Mike gazed up at the rim, and what his eyes saw might not have been registered by his mind. "We made mistakes, Nat, me bhoy. We been thinking those fellers came in down the track you went out by with the horses. We been thinking we had all the ways in taken care of. Leastways, Mike's been thinkin' so. Now, I'm for home and a drink."

"One shot of gelignite could break that ledge up there, and take care of this way down," Bony said, and Red nodded and said that would be done. "Anyway, we know now how those snoopers came into the valley, and how they went out."

"Yes, and I promised the women to take them to Bowral to do some shopping this afternoon. Come on!" moodily remarked Mike. "We'll go into all this again tomorrow."

Red was saying he remembered where there were a dozen dog traps they could set at likely places to catch a snooper, when they reached the settlement. The women were already dressed for what appeared to be a rare outing, and after lunch Mate Conway, Rosalie and three other women left in the truck, Mate Conway having Bony's measurements for new sports clothes to wear at the festival. When they returned they found Bony playing draughts with Grandma.

CHAPTER 21

Anniversary Eve

A s OFTEN happened, there was no rain this season, and Bony continued with the potato digging for another week. The deciduous trees, planted by the early settlers, had now lost their leaves, and the Australian stalwarts clung to their foliage and waited to shed their bark instead. The days were cold and sparkling. The heavy mists rolled into the valley early in the evening. Bony didn't know it, but the tang of Ireland pervaded Cork Valley.

Human activity gradually increased. Conway drove his truck to town every day, and the Kelly's green sedan often raised the dust of the snaking road to the rim. Bony wondered how often the bell indicator in Conway's house attracted the attention of the women.

The festival date was obviously drawing near, and when pressed by the children at table, Bony still failed to guess its name and nature. What did the eleventh of November enshrine in the hearts of these people? It wasn't Armistice Day, for he had seen no evidence of interest. Captain Cook didn't land at Botany Bay on this day of the year, and as far as he could recall, it wasn't William the Conqueror's birthday.

He had much to occupy his mind. He felt that at long last the Mountain was beginning to move towards him, and often he went back to that scene beyond the fall to capture the vocal nuances behind the words spoken by Mike Conway and Red Kelly.

It had obviously been the place where Eric Torby had entered Cork Valley those many months before. This was strongly supported by the evidence of a geologist's hammer having employed on the rock close to it. It could not have been a coincidence that the two snoopers had come down from the rim by the way taken by Torby. After leaving Cork Valley,

Torby hadn't lived long enough to inform anyone of that way down, and the only reasonable surmise was that the way down was known to the excise people or police before Torby had entered the valley. Unless, of course, there was a traitor among the men of Cork Valley.

What was the mistake admitted by Mike Conway, the mistake for which Red Kelly had refused to accept full responsibility? Bony soon realised it would be fruitless to ponder this question until something else could be associated with it, and for that to come his way he would need to be patient and alert.

The day following the incident, the boom of an explosion showed that his advice to destroy the ledge high above the floor of the valley had been taken. Subsequent blasting operations in other parts of the encircling mountains, denoted the blocking of other entrances to this rabbit burrow, and there was further evidence of unusual activity by the growing number of horses in the paddocks on the Kelly side of the wall.

The eleventh day of November was the anniversary day of the festival, but for some reason it had been advanced to July the first. It baffled Bony until he found that the likely answer was that the weather in November is clear, and that as fogs favoured the running of spiritous liquor, so the fogs would favour the celebrations of this festival to which everyone looked forward with increasing enthusiasm. He was certain that the withholding of its name was due only to their desire for him to guess, and since it was obvious to everybody else, his obtuseness was cause for merriment.

On the third day before the festival, everyone in Cork Valley became unusually busy. There were then two additional women at the home of the Conways, and about the other houses, Bony noted women and men he hadn't previously seen. More chimneys emitted smoke. More pigs were slaughtered and two fat bullocks were also killed behind the piggery.

Bony was asked to offside for Joe Flanagan, the settlement's electrician, and with Joe driving an old bomb of a utility, they inspected the bridges. Joe climbed under each of them and Bony handed him tools as required. He presented Joe with the screwdriver found in the water by the bridge and Joe said it was his favourite and was happy to have it again. There were more bridges than Bony thought, and he became engrossed when, with Joe, he fitted alarm points beneath old planks 'carelessly' laid across water gutters. Finally, miles of buried wiring had to be tested.

They got along well together, Joe finding Bony tireless and intelligent with tools, and never averse to tackling an awkward job. At midday they would light a fire and brew a billy of tea, and invariably Joe would produce his bottle for the pre-lunch swig. They would eat the sandwiches and cake provided, and spend an hour smoking and talking, sometimes of Joe's overseas tours, sometimes of Cork Valley and its people. Often Joe was loquacious; all reserve now vanished.

"Tomorrow, we finishes," he said, when driving home one evening. "Tomorrow we put in new batteries at all the base points, and then we fixes up the sign outside Red's house. After that we cleans our teeth and polishes our boots and gets ourselves ready for the shivoo." Momentarily, his grey eyes examined Bony. "Like a bit of advice?"

"Always open to advice."

"Eat hearty, for one thing, If you drink hard, eat hard."

"I shall do neither, except in moderation."

Joe laughed saying:

"When you see what's on the boards you'll never want to stop eating. I've seen the little 'uns looking at what there is, and crying because they can't eat no more." His voice softened. "For centuries the people of Ireland wellnigh starved. For centuries they lived in rags. And all to support the English landlords and the Government. A lot of 'em came out to Australia and starved, too, for years and years, in the old days. And after what they done, and what they suffered, this Cork Valley is the only bit of Ireland outside of Ireland."

"It's worth having," Bony said, and meant it.

"And it's the only decent God-fearing place in the country, too. We have our faults. We have our notions of justice. We believe in doing unto others, and the rest, and there's no more contented people in Australia."

"I can believe that, Joe. You said something of a sign outside Red's house. What sign?"

"Electric. We put it up outside his front entrance: The Glenrowan Hotel. Everyone sees it at night while the festival goes on and it could be for three days."

"The Glenrowan Hotel," repeated Bony. "That was the place where the Kelly gang came to a sticky end in 1880."

"That was it, Bony. As you reminded us at Red's house, it was the booze at the Glenrowan Hotel what betrayed Ned into his carelessness and he paid for it with his life. You spoke well of Ned Kelly. And you spoke true when you said he was crucified by the Irish." Joe sighed. "They're all dead now. But their friends pay their respects every year here in Cork Valley."

"In the dinkum Irish fashion, eh?"

"That's so, Nat. The kids get their chance to join in. The young folk can get on with their love making. The oldees can natter and gossip and tell tales. You're not going to forget it."

"Why, I think I could guess the name of the festival. It's called . . ."

"Don't guess now, Nat," urged Joe. "Guess when they ask you again at dinner."

Joe was right, but that night Bony's guesses were wilder than usual. They dined on Irish stew and for dessert there was bread and jam and cheese. It was the plainest meal Bony remembered, and, the cause was the imperative demands on the cooks by the preparations for the festival. There was an undercurrent of excitement, especially marked in the children, the only person unaffected being Rosalie who, since her visit to Bowral, was withdrawn. There had been no music practice since that day.

The next morning Joe and Bony conveyed to the big house a wide board studded with red reflectors to spell the name Glenrowan Hotel. This they affixed above the great entrance porch, and on the far side of the driveway a spotlight was rigged to a tree, Joe explaining that it would bring the sign into brilliance without producing light enough to be observed by anyone who might chance to be on the rim.

Where the road at the settlement turned to reach the Kelly house, they erected another sign reading: 'To Glenrowan'. For Bony this experience was unique. He whistled softly Irish airs. He noted the abnormal activities and the influx of strangers as a small boy watching a circus coming to town and helping to erect the tent. He forgot, for the time, Mahomet's Mountain, and the desirability of its approach to him. The responsibilities of his assignment became as light as thistledown—when he did remember them—whilst his career, with its rank and its importance of life was relegated to the chest where his Marie kept his uniform in tissue paper.

After lunch he and Joe went again to the big house in which the huge living-room or banqueting hall was in process of being wrecked. The tapestries had been removed and the grey walls were bare and ugly. Jack, the Smuggler, and two helpers were building a low stage across one corner. Red Kelly was superintending the introduction of the trunk of a tree to the ten-foot-wide open hearth. He was shouting to someone outside to "bar her in a bit more". As a dozen men could stand inside the fireplace, the tree trunk didn't look out of place although it was three feet thick.

Bony stood behind Red Kelly who was inside the fireplace, and he could see, beyond the opening at the side, the remainder of the tree extending outside the house, and two men employing crowbars to move the log on to iron rollers. The branches had been lopped off, and once the log was positioned, a boy could then nudge it into the fireplace with a light bar.

"How long is that going to last?" Bony asked, and Red stood to turn about, saw him, and shouted the answer.

" 'Bout a fortnight, Nat, just about, according what we use of her. None of your piddling stoves and 'lectric heaters for us. Heat is what we likes and heat is what we get. Nice stick of iron-bark, eh? I've had me eye on her these three years. Outside there's a mark on her put there by me grandfather in 1861. Have a look some time. We're going to burn history, Nat."

"History is painted on the walls, Red," declared a cracked

voice, and Bony saw a little old man with bright eyes in a weather-beaten face. He was wearing breeches and a coat like the one worn by Joe Flanagan, and on his white hair perched a top hat from which all the nap had long since been chewed by moths.

"Day to ye, Gaffer," roared Red. "Glad to see ye. How's the pison treating you?"

" 'Tis me liver, Red," replied Gaffer. "But if I go easy on the Dew then me sciatica gives me bloody blue hell."

Bony was beckoned by his boss, and with Joe he worked at rigging strings of lights beneath the ceiling.

"Can't see where Red booted a hole in it. Can you, Nat?"

"No. Red did a good job of repair work," and Joe chuckled at a memory he wanted to keep to himself.

Brian and two girls were nailing a huge Eireann flag on to one bare wall and on the opposite side of the room men were building what looked like a bar counter, and others were building shelves against that wall. Several boys began bringing in chairs all of the one pattern, and now and then through the rear door there came the aroma of beef being gently barbecued, and pastry being baked. The ancient in the top hat went out that way, like Cassius, with a lean and hungry look.

Bony found himself standing with Brian and his girls, admiring the flag tacked to the wall. One girl said it wasn't level, and the other agreed with Brian that it was. Men staggered in under the weight of the school piano, and Brian gave one of the girls his hammer while he went to assist them. Someone shouted and the girl dropped the hammer to the floor and Bony retrieved it. They were having trouble with the piano and he slipped the handle of the hammer down inside his belt and lent a hand.

The chaos was invaded by a dozen young lassies. Several carried cups with circular hoops passed through the handles. Others brought trays of buttered scones and tarts and cakes, and two boys appeared carrying a dixie of tea. Aged about twelve, they shyly served the workers with afternoon tea, and even Gaffer enjoyed the tea, having his cup refilled a dozen times. Afterwards, Bony accompanied Joe to the upstairs rooms where the light bulbs were tested and some replaced. Here women were making up beds. They noted him, slyly or openly, with interest. These rooms were without floor coverings, and only a few of them contained more than the beds: sometimes singles, often doubles.

They had to go out to the rear to fix outside lights, and what Bony saw there astonished him. Two whole bullocks were being barbecued. Three great boilers were emitting steam and the aroma of cooking hams and bacon. At the back of an open-fronted shed stared the fronts of baking ovens. And at the rear of all this stood a line of old and new cars, buggies and traps and buckboards.

The electricians' work done, Bony was asked to join the workers at the counter. They were nailing down the top.

"Time's a-knocking," said a slim, pale-faced man with a great shock of dark hair under a tam-o'-shanter. "Nails here. Ram in a few at your end of these boards."

Bony nodded, and looked about for a hammer, and was told there was one in his belt. He used this with good effect, and soon the job was accomplished, and the men turned to complete the shelves.

All was uproar and banging and voices. Dusk came, and Joe turned on the new lights to aid the old ones. The shelves were finished, and a cable was strung from wall to wall to support floor to ceiling curtains of bright green which would banish the counter from the rest of the room.

Then it was time to return to the settlement and dinner, and Bony put his hammer down with the other tools on the lid of a chest. Although it seemed an impossible fluke, on the handle, which the palm of his hand had been gripping for more than an hour, were carved the letters E.T.

Picking it up, he walked out openly with it and climbed into Joe's utility.

Coincidence! The thought occupied his mind still when he sat at the dining-table. Then his attention was distracted by Joe's neighbour, the red-headed boy.

"Come on, Nat! You have to guess the name of the festival."

"Have I? Now let me think. I know. The Fiddlers' Festival."

"No," chorused the children, and tonight were not checked by Mike Conway.

"Well, then, is it called the Ned Kelly Festival?"

"Yes," they shrieked, and Inspector Bonaparte laughed with them.

CHAPTER 22

The Skeleton at the Feast

DRESSED IN his smart new sports clothes and black shoes, purchased with money earned by digging spuds, Inspector Bonaparte was present at the official opening of the Ned Kelly Festival.

The gathering in the great hall of Red Kelly's mansion comprised not less than a hundred and fifty people, including children of all ages. The majority were sombrely dressed, and very few had obeyed the dictates of the current fashions, many of the women wearing costumes of bygone eras, while the men wore suits of mid- or late-Victorian vintage. But the cloth was of a high quality, and if the men scorned wrist-watches, their stomachs were decorated with heavy gold chains. It was a church congregation rather than a festival crowd.

Mike Conway made his way through the throng to the orchestra stage. He was wearing a black suit, with a snowy white shirt and inch-long white sleeve-cuffs. His black curly hair contrasted sharply with his pale complexion, and as he stood facing the audience seated in rows and standing massed at the sides, it was obvious that he had something of great importance to say. His dark eyes roamed over the people for half a minute before he spoke, and all impressions of him received by Bony were to be confirmed.

"It is good for us all to be joined again in a community spirit which has continued from its conception, in the days when life was indeed hard, down to the present, when we enjoy comparative luxury in living conditions and are still imbued with the faith and the ideals of our forefathers. They rebelled against oppression and fought for freedom. We are rebels against oppression, and we fight on for freedom. Without faith, without ideals we would have become as the morons in the cities who are satisfied as long as they are provided with bread and games as were the slaves in Roman days."

A good beginning, thought Bony, and was to have this first opinion qualified by reservations and differing views. Mike declared that the people of Cork Valley and the adjoining mountains were oppressed by the seven governments, plus the two thousand politicians, ruling Australia's population of a meagre ten million. He stressed the point that this small population was forced to support internal and external government agencies on a par with the great nations of a hundred millions and more. He stated as a fact that two thousand politicians, plus five thousand top civil servants, were battening on the producers. They received enormous salaries, were provided with perks covering every possible need for themselves and their families; the highest of them were given world tours, taking with them their wives and children, with secretaries and valets and maids, and the lowest managed to take long holiday tours in the north of Australia when the weather was cool, all paid for by the unfortunate taxpayers.

"It is said," he went on, "that you can do anything provided it is legal. These scoundrels have made it legal to rob the people. In the days of the great empires similar scoundrels looted and robbed without troubling to make their thieving legal. In those historic times the robbers were titled Caesars and Emperors: today they are Presidents and Cabinet Ministers. It matters not by what they are called; all are the same today as they were two thousand years ago; with the difference that for every parasite the people had to support in ancient times, we have to support fifty."

Mike paused to allow this remarkable assertion to sink in. Then coldly deliberate, he said:

"There have been many great tragedies in human history. The greatest tragedy of them all was the failure of a man named Guy Fawkes. Had Guy Fawkes succeeded in blowing up the English Parliament, the politicians even down to this day would have less contempt for the people they oppress . . . legally.

"We may not do anything which isn't legal, but we may

do anything at all which we consider to be moral. Morality is a greater power than legality. Thus we hold ourselves morally justified in resisting unmoral taxes. We are morally responsible for continually struggling to retain the last small vestiges of freedom left to us. As exemplars, I give to you the original Kellys. I call on our own Red Kelly."

Instead of wild cheers, there were respectful murmurs of sincere agreement, and then Red Kelly stood, his small blue eyes glinting in the subdued daylight, and the large mouth opening slowly amid the mass of fiery whiskers. Coming after the low voice of Conway, his words pounded on their ears.

"Kelly! Ned Kelly! The greatest Irishman of all toime. We all know about him, rest his soul. We all know how he fought back the police. We all know how his mother and sister, his brothers and himself were persecuted until he took up arms against the persecutors. They declared war on him and his, and he proved how great an Irishman he was by fighting back. He opened the banks and gave the money to the poor. The enemy locked up his mother without a trial, and his sister Kate, and many of their friends. Held 'em in durance for months and years. We know how they got Ned in the end. They got him not because they had guts and brains, 'cos they had neether, but because Ned and his gang had a party at the Glenrowan Hotel and weren't expectin' the enemy on the doorstep. So they shot it out with the police, and the police fired the hotel without mercy for the many unoffending people inside."

Groans came from the congregation, and Red Kelly produced a sheet of paper and held up a hand for silence.

"Now we could forget and forgive if the enemies of the Kellys had been English or Scotch, or German or Chinese. But, friends, the Kellys' antagonists were Irish, damn their eyes. Here is a list of 'em, the bastids who was paid blood money for murderin' their own countrymen. Listen here! I'll give you their names: Thomas Curnow, Constable Kelly, Stanhope O'Connor, Sergeant Whelan, Constable P. Kelly, Constable Dwyer, Constable Ryan, Constable Reilly, Constable Cawsey, Constable Healey, Constable Mullane, Constable McColl, Constable Meager, Constable . . . Ar, why go on. They all took their blood money, the dirty Irish bastids.''

The echoes of Red's voice faded into the silence, and the silence was broken by a unified yell of horror. The reaction of the listeners convinced Bony that this was a new line to them. Red continued:

"We know that after the last great fight at the Glenrowan Hotel Dan Kelly and Steve Hart were dead, and Ned Kelly severely wounded. We know that the people in the hotel were fired on, although they had nothing to do with the fight. We know how his Riverence Bishop Gibney went into the burning building and, in spite of the police fire, brought out people and saved them from death. And we know how Ned was tried, before ever he was took to court, before Judge Barry, and how Judge Barry condemned him to death, and then went home and died of a foul disease, smitten down by the God of Justice he had offended.''

Red glared at the meeting, and the meeting groaned and rocked. He looked about till he found Bony, and then dramatically pointing, said:

"There's a heathen what has become a Conway. I tell you now of Nat Bonnay, my friend and my conqueror. He named us a name. He calls the Irish in government and departments as no good bastid Irish, and us he names the dinkum Irish. We are dinkum Irish and proud of it. Thank you Nat for speakin' true. Now come up here and say a word before I call on Gaffer to open the festival.''

Not unprepared because Red had threatened to call on him to address the gathering, Bony stepped to the platform and smiled all round, ending with Grandma Conway. They smiled back at him, and he knew then that for the first time in his life he was free of the colour bar. He said:

"I will not make a speech. I will, however, recite a poem written by an old friend of mine. This is how it goes:

"In days of old, when men were bold,
    The Kellys roamed the scrub.

They flitted about from bank to bank,
    And finished up at the pub."

Doubtful of the reaction to this, Bony went on to the next verse of the ode:

"The police couldn't tell what Ned would do,
    Nor when and how he'd act.
In the broad of day or the dark of night,
    He'd give to the lean and take from the fat!"

The audience stirred, looking one at another, beginning to smile, and Bony went on courageously:

"The times were bad in those faraway days,
    And the Irish were split in twain.
The ill-born bastards served the Queen,
    The gintlemen Kellys never drew rein."

Men cheered and women clapped, delaying the next verse.

"Ned's old mother they flung into gaol,
    They couldn't catch Ned, so took her instead.
With never a trial nor beg pardon to her,
    They kept her in gaol till Ned lost his head.

"And now my friends all the tale is told,
    Of the Fight for Justice in the days of old.
They took poor Ned and dropped him deep,
    And all dinkum Irish will his memory keep."

Probably in relief from Mike Conway's theology and Red Kelly's harangue, the audience was vociferous in its applauding of Bony's poetry. Bony would have enjoyed his reward had not Red, in joyous mood, clapped him on the back and winded him. Then Gaffer was being introduced as the oldest inhabitant, and he began to speak, with his top hat still mounted. He was terse, merely saying he was honoured to open the Ned Kelly Festival.

Immediately orderly attention gave place to seeming chaos. Men and women left the room. Others rearranged the chairs.

Others erected trestle tables. Children looked expectant. They were marched to the stage by Rosalie, and there sang grace in the sudden hush. The silence of the throng continued after the voices ceased, and everyone was still and waiting.

This was outside Bony's experience. The people were solemn: the setting almost drab with the daylight entering through the three tall windows. Old Gaffer leaned on his stick and gazed on the children. His absurd coat made him look like a kind of beetle, and the top hat was like a chimney pot bashed by a gale. Mike Conway's brother reclined amidst his pillows and cushions, and standing beside his cot was Jack the Smuggler. There was Grandma Conway in her high-back chair, wearing a green silk gown and lace cap, and with her were several ancient women, like ladies-in-waiting to the Matriarch of Cork Valley.

From beyond the rear doorway came the roll of a drum, quickening in tempo and ending abruptly. The low wailing of the warpipes became loud and louder when the piper entered the great room playing the 'Wearing o' the Green'. He headed a procession of white-garbed cooks bearing huge platters and dishes laden with turkeys, broiled pigs' heads, huge hams, piles of vegetables, whole cheeses, thick rich cream and fruit pies. The piper led the cooks about the room and between the tables and the people seemed lifted up by the spiritual force which captured Bony, of the Australian inland. The strings of lights he and Joe had arranged flashed on, and all was colour and sudden laughter. The Ned Kelly Festival had begun.

Bony suddenly felt a little isolated, a stranger in this hundred per cent Irish gathering. Neither by right of birth nor national sympathies could he ever be one with these sparkling people of the mountains. He failed to wipe from his mind the purpose of his presence here, or expunge from his consciousness the feeling of guilt. It needed effort to remember his assignment, to remember who he was and what he was. A hand was placed on his arm, and a voice said:

"So it's you who crush the ribs and half strangle innocent maidens on a mountain shelf in the dark of night. I see now what a fool I was to try and hit you for being fresh. Why, Nat, you're the loveliest man. Please take me to dinner."

"Why! 'Tis Bessie O'Grady! You remember me?"

"What girl wouldn't after what you did in the dark of night?"

She was wearing a flared skirt of bright green, a silk jacket of dark orange, and through her hair was laced a ribbon the colour of the skirt. Her eyes were big and shining and they banished the weather-ruined complexion. In them was mental strength and behind the smile a resolute character. The grip of her hand was powerful.

Urged forward, Bony escorted her to one of the serving tables where the cook said:

"Now for a nice slice of turkey flanked by a slice of Cork Valley ham?"

Arrayed in white coat and apron, and wearing a chef's hat, he wasn't instantly recognised as Mike Conway, and Bony excused himself on the ground of the unusual circumstances. He followed Bessie O'Grady, his platter heavy in his hands, and sat with her at the vacant end of a table. He became aware that she had piloted him there in order to talk of matters not associated with Cabbages and Kings.

"I posted the letter," she said.

"Did you!"

"Rosalie's breaking her heart."

"Oh! Why?"

"She's in love, Nat. That's why. Have you ever been in love?"

"Yes. It's always worrying at first."

"I haven't, so I don't know about it. Say something funny. Grandma's watching us."

"Have you told Brian that he's going to marry you?"

"Not yet, Nat," replied Bessie, and managed to laugh. "I'm getting worried over Rosalie. I slept with her last night, and she showed me the letter he wrote, in the book, and told me what she had written to him. She asked him to send her a letter to the Bowral Post Office, and he never did. If ever I come up against him, I'll kick his face in."

"Now, Bessie," he said reprovingly. "That wouldn't be lady-like."

"Lady-like!" she said, keeping her face tilted down to her platter. "I'm no bloody lady, Nat. Go on, crown me with your dinner. Do something to stop me crying."

CHAPTER 23

Crumbs of Information

THE AFTERNOON was given up to the children and their parents, the older people drifting into groups and many volunteering to deal with the dishwashing and the catering. When Bony offered to help with these chores he was reminded that he was a member of the orchestra.

Not all the children, of course, were Rosalie's pupils. Many had come from outside, and one group, led by a stooped, white-haired ascetic, gave several one-act plays. As actors they were quite good, and someone told Bony that the plays had been presented for years.

Before backstage drops, incidents in the lives of the Kelly gang were enacted on the temporary stage. Two girls played Mrs Kelly and her daughter Kate busy at home tasks, and several boys were 'policemen', uniformed in the style of that era. They invaded the cottage and submitted the women to abuse and bullying. Another scene portrayed the arrival of the gang at Jerilderie and the locking up of the policeman, while Ned Kelly took the policeman's wife to church while the local bank was being stripped of cash. Yet another scene showed young Ned being bashed by policemen for stealing a horse he swore he knew nothing about. Then an old plough was placed on the stage and the Kellys held a conference on how to use the shares to make suits of body armour to deflect the bullets fired at them by the police. Finally, to every boy and girl, Conway's invalid brother presented a costly present.

Following the children's session everyone did whatever they wished. On the line of tables against one wall meats and sweets and drinks awaited the hungry and thirsty. As night blacked out the windows, the orchestra started up, and Bony, with his gum-leaf 'music', was blacked out by the massed accordions and fiddles. For a couple of hours the dancing was non-stop, and the first break was given over to a singer with a magnificent tenor voice, and a solo by Bony who played 'Danny Boy'.

About eleven o'clock that night, Grandma Conway retired with her ladies-in-waiting, and many of the women also departed. The younger women stayed, dancing and flirting with fellows of their own age group.

By this hour Bony was beginning to feel slightly the worse for wear despite rigid economy on Mountain Dew. He found it impossible to refuse a noggin with Gaffer, and it wasn't possible to decline to join Red Kelly in a drink or two over supper. Red was uproarious. He danced with all the girls with an *élan* equal to that of his son Brian. Then he sat on the floor with his back to a wall and slept for an hour, awoke, and began all over again.

Nothing that evening seemed to affect Bessie O'Grady. She demanded a dance with Bony, and although he found the dances difficult, she helped assiduously and then insisted on sitting out, bringing up again the subject of Rosalie's love affair.

"I think I'll kid Dad to let me go up to Sydney," she said. "He will if I work him right, and I'll chase that Eric Hillier and see if I can get any sense out of him. I can't just stay and watch poor Rosalie breaking her heart like she's doing."

"You think a lot of her, don't you?" Bony told her, deciding to test a line of action he had been thinking over. He was sure that Bessie's inordinate affection was based on an admiration of one so opposite and it was a trifle unbalanced. The girl swiftly nodded agreement, and her expression was one of almost fanatic adoration. He said: "Supposing Eric Hillier never received her letter?"

"But he did. I posted it myself in Kiama."

"Posting it doesn't mean that he received it. He might not have gone back to Sydney."

"But he must've," argued Bessie. "He lives at No. 10 Evian Street."

"Rosalie said that when he wrote to Mike Conway his address was some other place. Didn't she tell you that?"

"Yes." Bessie drank her 'wine', frowned, and was silent for several minutes. Then: "I don't like it, Nat. I've got to go to Sydney to find him and have it all out."

"Rosalie didn't see him leave Cork Valley, did she?"

Another period of silence followed the question.

"No, Rosalie didn't see him leave."

"Then why not find out who he went with? You could find that out, surely. Better start here in Cork Valley than rush about in Sydney."

They were sitting side by side at a table, and in a swift frenzy, the girl turned and gripped Bony by both arms, forcing him to confront her blazing eyes.

"What are you saying, Nat? Tell me. Go on, tell."

"You know as much as I do. I know very little, so you could know a great deal more. Supposing . . . I say supposing, Brian Kelly has been after Rosalie. Supposing he knew Rosalie had fallen for Eric Hillier, and supposing he had been told to take Eric Hillier out to Wollongong and the rail station there. How does that fit?"

Bessie relaxed her grip on his arms and snatched up her glass. He said:

"Don't drink any more. You want to serve Rosalie. So do I. We must keep our heads clear. We must find out who took Eric from Cork Valley—if he went at all. Now think hard. Supposing Hillier found out a secret of Cork Valley, or supposing he was reckoned as a rival and . . . well, you know. It comes to this, Bessie. We have to find out if Eric is alive or dead. If he's dead, we can't go on letting Rosalie think he's alive."

The girl was silent for several minutes, and Bony employed his fingers rolling cigarettes for her and himself. He had sown the seed and wondered what the plant would be, and he was to be kept wondering when Steve came to ask Bessie for a dance. He was not left alone. Mike Conway set a bottle on the table, and occupied Bessie's place.

"You seem to be having a good time, Nat. I hope you are." He was carrying his liquor well, and the hand which manipulated the bottle over their glasses was firm. "That Bessie

O'Grady should have been a man. Has she been working on you?"

"Yes, I believe she has." Bony raised his glass and paused to offer a toast. "Here's to the Festival," he said. "You know, Mike, I could be older than you, but you'll probably agree that old as we are we can count the ifs and imagine ourselves very different had we made wiser decisions in our early years. I'm game to bet that the man Bessie marries will find out she wants more than money. She'll want him to be Lord High Justice, or something, because what she makes him she'll make herself. Perhaps she thinks, without knowing it, of course, that I am the type of man she needs."

"To express herself in and through, you mean?"

"Yes. You know I did a lot of reading once. Found that almost all the great men in history were made great by their women. You read much?"

"Once, yes." Conway smiled although his eyes were speculative.

"I know what you're thinking," Bony said. "I'm a puzzle you can't solve. I'll solve it for you. I went to high school and to the Brisbane University. Then I went bush and became a horse-breaker and stockman. I held all the ace cards of life and played every one wrong. I am true to type. Just as you are. Your parents and their parents fashioned you. Mine have fashioned me. Tell me, why you aren't drunk, and I'll tell you why I am trying to keep sober."

"You ring a bell, Nat." Conway stared at Bony's glass from which he had taken merely a sip. "I'll think about the puzzle: perhaps give you the answer of the last puzzle, why we aren't as drunk as Red and many of the others. It could be that in our different ways we are both seekers after perfection."

"You might have gone further in the search than you think," Bony mused. "Here are all these people, your people. It's two o'clock in the morning. Most of them are drunk. Yet I haven't heard one obscene word, and never a hint that any woman might be offended. It isn't a result of the Mountain Dew."

"No, Nat, it is the result of training and disciplining a wholesome community. Those who can't be amendable to our standards are disgorged, cast out beyond the pale. There have been very few, but still a few." Again there was speculation in Mike's dark eyes. "This community was first established and has been maintained on the axiom of 'One for All and All for One'. Religion has been a powerful amalgam, but the ideal of truth and justice and simplicity of heart created in, not by, the Kelly gang has been a greater power of cohesion; thus this festival."

Bony smiled directly into Conway's probing eyes. Lifting his glass, he said:

"Let's drink to it, properly."

Mike laughed, raised his glass and touched, saying:

"Now continue easy, Nat. The night's still a child and all."

The night's age was doubtful. On the platform was left but one fiddler. He was accompanying the tenor. The singer was weaving. His eyes were shut and no sound came from his working mouth. When the fiddler stopped playing and rose to accept the acclaim of an indifferent audience, the singer maintained his mouth action as he pitched forward off the platform and was caught by Jack who lowered him to the floor and left him to join in a small private singing party. Above the hubbub Red Kelly roared:

"Hey, Mac, get outsoid and do a bit of barring. The fire's nigh dead on us."

Red was terrific. He towered over the young woman clinging to his arm, and she was no delicacy. Her hair was disarrayed and in colour matched his. His whiskers flamed like the rays of a sun, and he was eating from a whole ham from which little had previously been carved. Brian was leading a choir seated on the floor, and beside him was Bessie with one arm about his neck and her mouth close to his right ear.

"Better start to break it up," Mike said and stood.

Bony weaved through small groups and stepped over bodies, to arrive before the huge fireplace and be fascinated by the tree creeping in through the hole beside the hearth. The man outside wanted to know 'how she was a-coming', and presently Bony decided 'she' had come far enough. With a long-handled shovel he scooped the glowing embers about the end of the log, and was then entranced by an extraordinary scene.

Mike Conway was going from woman to woman. To each he smiled, saying something Bony couldn't catch, and without demur they smiled in return and left the room. The man's influence was notable. On pausing before Red's companion, the giant shouted that it was time enough yet for the women to retire, but the woman laughed up at him, withdrew her arm from his, smiled at Mike, and obediently left. Red started to shout at Mike, but Conway merely turned from him and approached Bessie. Bessie waved gaily to those still on their feet and ran after the red-haired woman.

The departure of the women was merely an incident. Some of the musicians assembled on the platform and began to play. Men came with wicker clothes-baskets and gathered empty bottles and discarded glasses. Every bottle bore the label of a well-known brand of whisky, but it was far in the past when they contained anything so wishy-washy as whisky. Bony remarked on this to a gangling tough in his Sunday-go-Meeting clothes, and was told that refreshment was always poured from legitimate whisky bottles in case of a raid.

"Had one five-six years back," the ruffian said, smiling and revealing the residue of front teeth. "Police walked in on us. They looked at the bottles, held 'em to the light, left 'em. Nothing illegal entertaining guests on whisky."

He possessed the rare distinction of having one eye brown and the other blue. He was as drunk as a fiddler's bitch, but could still see straight.

"That was a fine poem you gave us, Nat. Will ye be doing it again on the morrow?"

"Yes, if I'm asked. What's your name, by the way? I've seen you before."

"Me! Oh, I'm Tim O'Halloran. I'm on this side of the wall, Nat. Anything to say agin it?"

"I will if the wall should stop us drinking together," laughed Bony, and they 'walked' to a table where they opened a bottle of the best Scotch . . . in name. "Well, here's to a thick ear before morning, Tim. You know, you defeat me. Wait a moment, though. I remember. You were the fellow who found that Hillier man mooching about over by the fall."

"Yes, that's me, Nat, that's me. Said he was a geologist. Said he was hoping to find a trace of gold. Never believed it."

"Course not," Bony agreed. As Tim was not as yet ready to lie down on the verge of a black-out, Bony airily switched from the subject to one less dangerous. "I'm going to cut myself a snack. Coming?"

O'Halloran chose to nurse the bottle, and broke into song. Bony cut himself a sandwich of pickled pork and smeared it heavily with mustard. An abstemious man, he was fighting against the Dew, and marvelled at himself for still being upright. Carrying the sandwich, which looked like a paving-stone, he weaved out through the rear door and to the kitchen where he discovered an enormous woman standing at a vast cooking range.

"Now what is it ye want? Git out of me kitchen," she shouted. "You men ain't allowed here."

"Now don't be after being angry me darlin'," he pleaded. "It's a cup or two of tea I'm lookin' for. I'm perishing from the thirst."

"'Well, get along out and perish in a corner. There's no tea nor coffee brewed at three in the morning. You're no Irish anyway. You're . . . "

"I'm Nat Bonnay, sweet. And I must have a gallon or two of tea. Now, don't be violent wid me. I tell you what. I'll play on me gum leaf for you. Listen!"

Dropping the sandwich to the table, he produced a leaf. The house cook advanced one, two steps, towards him. She halted, swayed on her great slippered feet, and he played as though inspired 'Where the River Shannon Flows'. Her dark eyes began to gleam. Her vast bosom heaved under the gaudy dressing-gown, and when the last of the reedy notes left their echo in her ears she said:

"Sit ye down, Nat, and I'll brew ten gallons of tea for ye."

CHAPTER 24

The Grand Parade

HER NAME was Nora O'Connor. Her weight was probably eighteen stone. Her red hair was now white, her nose bulbous, her mouth was her most mobile feature, expressing mirth, anger, sympathy or coyness with express speed. She said she was up early to prepare breakfast for all the guests who asked for it.

Having been serenaded with Danny Boy, she asserted:

"Tea revives you; coffee sustains you. What'll it be?"

Bony chose coffee when remembering there was another day round the corner, and observing that a huge coffee pot was emitting an enticing aroma from the stove. His head was clear, but his eyes burned and his throat was raw. The price he had paid for being a detective was indeed high. He was told to sit at the central table, and then this paragon of a cook regarded his sandwich with extreme aversion, picked it up between thumb and finger as though it were a dead rat, and tossed it into a scrap pail.

"You shall be ating of bacon and eggs and buttered toast," she said. "Between sips of your coffee you can play that tune agin. Or another if you knows 'em."

The coffee was special. The bacon began sizzling in the pan. Bony was astonished by the economy of movement with which she prepared his breakfast. He played 'Danny Boy', and hoped that Grandma Conway wouldn't hear and become jealous. He played it again as the coffee began to bring back a feeling of physical well-being, he being one of the unfortunates whom alcohol does not exhilarate. Having eaten, he said he would go home to sleep for a couple of hours, but Nora wouldn't hear of it, and showed him to a cell-like room furnished with a single bed and ordered him to 'hop in'.

On waking he found Bessie O'Grady standing beside the bed and offering a tray of tea and toast.

"Time to rise and shine, Nat."

"What is the time, Bessie?"

"Gone ten o'clock. You should of taken your shoes off."

Sitting with his feet to the floor and the tray on his knees, he smiled up at her, and failed to bring an answering smile. Her eyes were angry, but he knew it was not with him. She said:

"Everyone's doing their chores about the place, and getting ready for dinner. Eric Hillier left the settlement with Brian Kelly. It was late afternoon, and school was still in. That's why Rosalie didn't see him go. Some time before lunch, they'd like you to join in with the orchestra for a session. Feeling all right?"

"Wonderful," he told her.

"You will feel even better after a short hair of the dog. I did. I found out something else. Brian Kelly didn't come back in their car. He walked back."

"What time?"

"I don't know. Red drove the car home first thing next morning. You eat that toast now. I cut out the butter. Dry toast will settle your stomach. Dad will let me go to Sydney some time. See you later."

Still unsmiling, Bessie left, and Bony sat on and smoked several cigarettes before asking Nora for a towel and borrowing a razor from Jack the Smuggler.

Signs of the festivities of the previous day had been removed from the great room when Bony entered it. He found nearly all the women gathered about Grandma Conway before the huge fireplace, and the children playing with their toys on the floor. The orchestra—two fiddles and three accordions—was playing softly, and he joined them. Rosalie wasn't at the piano and she wasn't among the women.

The interlude was terminated by the entry of several men who came to arrange the tables for dinner, and by the women who collected the new generation and took it off for a scrub. Noon passed, and other men drifted in, and again there was that pause of expectancy heralding the coming of the piper leading the procession of cooks.

Following this second enormous meal further sketches and playlets were presented by the children. One was grim, indeed. It began with a police party commanded by a sergeant making camp, and the reconnoitring of this party by one of the Kellys at a place named Stringybark Creek. The Kellys attacked and the sergeant and two constables were shot, the third constable getting away in a vast hurry. This was actually the first clash between the gang and police, the latter suffering ignoble defeat. Long and persistent persecution had thus ended in open warfare which was to continue until the horrific affair at Glenrowan.

Glenrowan was a small township on the new railway from Melbourne, and the Gang had planned to stop a train one mile on the Melbourne side of Glenrowan. It was intended to give a false alarm to the many police reinforcements on the train, and when they rushed to the local barracks thinking the Kellys were holding the local police there, the train was to move on to Glenrowan with all their horses. The horses were to be detrained and driven away into the hills, leaving the police stranded, and all the banks north of Glenrowan just so many sitting ducks.

A June Sunday in 1880 was the D-Day. There were two hotels then at Glenrowan, one being run by a Kelly friend, and the other by a Mrs Jones, a Kelly enemy. The friendly publican was left alone. Mrs Jones was forced to receive the Gang who herded into her hotel most of the Glenrowan population. A great day eventuated for everyone, excepting Mrs Jones who watched her provender and liquor being distributed in a grand party, and there were sports for the children in the back yard during the afternoon. The Gang became befuddled with drink, and the train wasn't halted until right at Glenrowan, when the police surrounded the hotel and at once began firing into it without regard for the Gang's innocent hostages within. As the walls were of flimsy wood, their bullets went straight through. Thus was the hatred of the police, half of whom were Irish, for the Kellys who had held them to ridicule for a year.

Glenrowan! Three of the Gang died at Glenrowan, and the

fourth was hanged. At Glenrowan was extinguished the last spark of rebellion against autocratic bureaucracy.

Glenrowan! The curtains across one side of Kelly's hall were drawn aside to reveal the bar of a hotel, and against the shelves at the back, loaded with bottles, was suspended a sign: 'The Glenrowan Hotel'. A man in shirt sleeves, wearing a scarlet waistcoat, was languidly washing glasses. A cat was cleaning itself at one end of the counter. A woman appeared, tall and angular, dressed in the style of the 1880's. She entered from the side and began to berate the barman for loafing on the job.

Two men entered the room. One was wearing a frock coat and black whiskers. The other wore drain-pipe trousers, a high-buttoned coat and a huge cravat in which was stuck a great golden horseshoe. They nodded to Mrs Jones and called for rum and milk. They were quaffing this mixture when from outside there came the rising thunder of approaching horses. Into the room sprang a youth to shout:

"The Kellys are here!"

The youth disappeared. Mrs Jones swooned. The customers vaulted the counter and, with the barman, disappeared.

From outside came the mumble of many voices, the low commands of men, and the clanking of metal. In from both front and rear doors came the people of Glenrowan: Rosalie and Bessie, Gaffer and Grandma, in her chair, and the invalid Conway pushed along in his cot by Mrs Conway. They came in like a driven herd of cattle. And after them came men in armour.

There were four of them. Their armour was built of steel ploughshares bolted together to provide protection for body and shoulders and a helmet for the head. The leader was a giant. He carried a rifle and an ancient revolver. He could see through the narrow slit level with his eyes, and as there was no mouth opening his voice boomed as though from the depth of a cavern.

"Ho, there, Mrs Jones," he called to the woman who had recovered from her swoon. "Begone to your room, Mrs Jones, and stay there or be shot." He pounded the bar counter and ordered the barman to come up from under. "Drinks, me bhoy! Drinks for all the guests of the Kellys this day." His ice-blue eyes flickered beyond the slit in his helmet. "The day is ours, people. Drink and make merry for you're the guests of the Kellys. At Ma Jones' expense."

Bony, with the other members of the orchestra, had watched this re-creation of history with astonishment. The crowd surged towards the bar. The two 'customers' bobbed up and assisted the barman to dispense orders. And with his fellow musicians, he, too, breasted the bar.

The giant leader roared and shouted and cheered on the guests. Beneath the chin lap of the helmet sprouted black whiskers. The voice was strange, disguised by the metal. But the black whiskers were at odds with the red hairs on the back of his great hands.

"To hell with it. I can't drink," he shouted, and lifted off the helmet to reveal Red Kelly. His gang copied him, betraying Smuggler Steve, Brian Kelly and Tim O'Halloran. After their electrifying entrance, they now looked a trifle ridiculous.

Men leaned against the bar, some of them wearing false whiskers and others clothes of the old days when the Kellys roamed the scrub. Old Gaffer was so excited that more grog slipped down his chin than down his throat. The children were given beakers of 'soft' drink, and two of them clung to Ned Kelly's massive legs with expressions of adoration on their chubby faces.

The place was packed, there being more people present than at any previous moment of this festival. The lights were flashed on. The air was heavy with tobacco smoke, and the uproar was endless. Again night came. Again the side tables were loaded with viands and again here and there a man floundered to sit with his back to a wall and close his eyes.

Still in his body armour, but minus his helmet, one of these was Brian Kelly. He leaned his head against the cool wall, and was drifting into unconsciousness when he heard as from a distance the voice of Nat Bonnay.

"What a show, Brian! What a shivoo! You can't go to sleep yet. Here, I've brought you a drink to toast Old Ireland with."

"Don' wanna no more," protested Brian, keeping his eyes closed. Nat Bonnay shouted with laughter, drank, spilled Mountain Dew down inside Brian's steel armour, laughed again, and said:

"Nothing like this where you're going, Brian."

"Where I'm going? You tell me. Think I'm going to London and Dublin? Like hell. I'm staying to chase Rosalie, Nat. She's ma girl. I'm having Rosalie if it's the last thing . . ."

"Sez you," sneered Nat Bonnay. "She's still nuts on that Hillier feller."

"Don' care, Nat. She'll forget him in time. He's in Sydney. I'm right here. Wanna go to sleep. Leave me alone."

He heard Nat Bonnay chuckling. He felt the rim of a glass against his lips, and drank. Good chap, Nat. Fight like a demon, boots and all, but a good feller at heart. He heard Nat say, chuckling again:

"But you bumped him off, didn't you? You had the chance. You must have taken the chance to fix him."

"Bloody fool!" muttered Brian Kelly. "Not you, Nat, not you. Me. I shoulda bumped him off. The old man reckoned I might of. He took him off me and sent me back."

"Did he now?"

"Don' worry, Nat. Everything's jake. I'll marry that Rosalie. Betcha."

There was a long silence, within the noise compounded of shouts, laughter, music, and a man singing with powerful voice, 'Come Back to Erin'.

"You might at that, Brian." The voice of Nat Bonnay came from the back of beyond. "Yes, you might at that. Where was it your old man took Hillier over from you?"

"Shut up, Nat. Wanna sheep."

"Up on the rim, I suppose."

"Beyond Conway's house. Up where the track joins the main road. Stopped us. Told me to get out. Said I was only a kid. Hit me with a spanner or something. Fix him before I'm ninety, Nat."

"I might take him off your hands, Brian. Nighty night."

CHAPTER 25

Dinkum Irish Frolics

Bony pretended to be overcome. He lay on his side, his head cradled in his arm, his back to the wall. Beneath his lowered lids he could see beyond the dancers, the hotel bar, the orchestra with Rosalie now playing the piano and the main front door. Red Kelly in his armour was seated on the end of the bar counter, roaring songs with several of his cronies. There could be no doubt of the toughness of these people of Cork Valley. Grandma was defying Mike who was urging her go to her room, and Bessie was dancing with her gaunt father. Not drunk enough to be deprived of his voice, the tenor was competing with Red Kelly.

The progress made during the last twelve hours was the direct result of the many weeks he had spent getting to know these people and studying them. In Casement's view, and he represented the over-all police opinion, these people of Cork Valley were an indivisible entity, a close-knit community within the larger community of a state. The opinion was only accurate to a limited degree, and Bony now believed he would soon prove it. The reward for diligence and patience was just around the corner. At the end of another hour, under the influence of Mountain Dew, many of those still on their feet would be amenable to an exchange of confidences.

Despite her protests, Grandma was taken from the scene. Almost stealthily, Rosalie left the piano and made her exit. Bessie saw her on the way to the rear door, but her dancing partner refused to release her. Bessie was high.

Bony permitted himself to regain consciousness. Sitting up he yawned at Joe Flanagan who was doing an Irish jig, all by himself, stretched his arms and tested his feet. Among the crowd at the bar was Steve, and Steve's face wore a fixed grin because those about him seemed oblivious of him and he was feeling lonely. He welcomed Bony, clutching at his shoulders to keep himself standing.

"Good ole Nat! How ya doin', Nat?"

"Just had a sleep and ready to start again, Steve." Bony shouted to one of the barmen, and they were instantly served. "Party's going well. Best party I ever been to, Steve. Red's on top of his form, eh? No troubles on his mind."

"As you said, he hasn't got a mind."

Bony turned and leaned against the counter. He smiled at Steve and the reserved Steve now grinned with genuine warmth.

"Pity he don't retire," he said, referring to Red. "One day ²'s going to make a real serious mistake, and some of us will find ourselves in goal. It's why I spoke my mind. Mike's something again. He does know how to add up."

Steve placed an affectionate hand on Bony's arm, saying:

"You know, Nat, me and you could run the trips without any worry at all, at all."

"What I don't like, Steve, is worry when it isn't necessary. I wouldn't want pistols on the job, would you?" Steve shook his head, found it hurt, winced and agreed. Another drink, perhaps, could complete the sedative action. Bony asked for refills. "About the silliest thing I ever heard of was that Kelso affair."

"Yes. An' nothin' to do with us, neether. You know about that, Nat?"

"Well, you told me, didn't you?"

"Did I?" Steve frowned heavily, drank deep. "I don't..."

"Well, why try to remember anyway? This isn't a quiz session." Bony laughed with spontaneous humour. "I reckon that armour suits you. Who are you in the play?"

"Dan Kelly. Bit heavy, but got more actin' to do. Yes, that Kelso job was crook, a private argument holding up business like it did. Like it did, Nat. Can't mix business with pleasure. The Kellys' pleasure: our business. Lose their blocks. Don't know their own strength. A killing to smooth out. Here, let me sit down. There's three of you. Bad sign, and I got more actin' to do."

Bony was almost pulled to the floor, but managed to prop Steve into a corner. Steve was now ripe.

"Red'll kill someone else 'fore he's through," Bony said.

"Tole Mike if he did I wouldn't live no more in Cork Valley."

"What did Mike say?"

"Said if Red did, it's the open country for him, not me nor anyone else. Gimme a drink?"

"You've had it, Steve. Have a sleep. I'll be standing by."

A long dry chuckle met Bony as he straightened up from arranging Steve, and there was Gaffer under the top hat, eyes bright and twinkling.

"Weak. That's what they are, Nat," he averred. "Not like my generation. Not like Dan Kelly he's supposed to be. How are you farin'?"

"All right, so far. How are you?"

"Some way off from being like him, Nat," replied Gaffer. He was gazing appreciatively at Bony when in through the open front door ran a boy to stand gaping at the scene until he saw Red Kelly sitting on the counter. Darting in and out between the dancers, he pushed his way through the men about Kelly, and shouted: "The police ... " He was so excited or so winded, he appeared likely to collapse and had to fight for coherence. "The police are on the way, Red. True, Red."

Red Kelly ceased his shouting, glanced at the ancient clock at the back of the bar, and roared with laughter.

"You're too early, Col, too early. Come back in half an hour. Go on, git away now. I'm telling you, bhoy."

"But, Red, true, Red."

"Get to hell wid ye. I'm a-talking. Run him out, Ed."

A stocky man hurried the protesting boy to the door, thrust him outside and closed the door. He was laughing when he returned and Red was continuing his tale of a stray steer. From the short incident, Gaffer looked direct to Bony, and Bony said:

"Was that in the act?"

The old man nodded, clearly puzzled, and said: " 'Tis in the play actin', Nat; as Red said, a trifle early."

"Then the boy's a good actor."

"Could be too good, Nat. Could be a trifle too good. I'll go an have a word with him."

"I'll go with you. Wonder where Mike is."

"Pacifying Grandma, seems like. Only level head here."

"How you going, Gaffer, you bloody immortal?" yelled Red Kelly as they were skirting his group. "Any toime you want a wrestle, Nat, just give a hint or two."

Bony smiled and winked and followed Gaffer. Then Bessie was holding him by the arm and saying:

"Dance with me, Nat. I've got something. They burned his clothes and things in the kitchen range the morning after."

"Just a moment Bessie. There's something we have to look into."

They didn't reach the front door. It was flung inward and four large men entered, lining up to confront the crowd. They wore raincoats over civilian suits, but they had that unmistakable appearance. The gyrating people halted. Red and others damped their voices, became silent and tense. One of the four said loudly:

"Excise officers here. Have a warrant to search the place. Running a bar, eh? Well, well! Good day's come at last."

No one moved, save Red Kelly who slowly slid off the counter, and as slowly put on his sinister helmet.

The leader of the intruders laughed but without mirth.

"Ned Kelly to the life. And he's actually dyed his whiskers black. What a yarn to tell the kids. What . . ."

His voice was drowned out by the skirl of the war-pipes and in by the rear door marched the piper playing 'It's a great day for the Irish'. The crowd opened to let him through. A powerful man, he strode across the room, seemed to sweep Red Kelly from his path, came on and on to confront the leader of the invaders. He kicked the leader in the stomach, smartly about turned, and marched back leaving the man writhing on the floor. Other than these two no one moved until the piper had left the room. Red Kelly was the first to break the tableau.

The man on the floor continued to writhe. One of the remaining three bent over him. Another looked stupidly uncertain at the advancing armoured giant, and the fourth produced a revolver. Then Bony was nudged aside, having to take Bessie with him, and Mike Conway confronted the strangers. His voice was a whip.

"Who are you?"

"Excise officers. Stand back. We have a warrant."

"Show it."

"It'll be shown, mister. You stand back. Any rough stuff and I'll shoot."

"This is a private house. This is a private party," Mike said, coldly. "You will withdraw at once, this instant."

"Afterwards, Mr Conway, afterwards. I'll drop the first man who makes a move."

At Mike's side was Bony. Behind them were ranged a rampart of men. They concealed swift activity going on behind them. Bottles of whisky, alleged, were being tossed into a shaft behind the bar counter, and bottles of real whisky placed thereon. Bony did not know of this. He was burning with anger.

Now the leader was recovering; he managed to speak, telling his man with the revolver to shoot if attacked. A moment later he resumed command.

"You men move back."

The four men moved forward, but Mike and Bony and those behind budged not an inch, resulting in two absurdly immovable objects. The excise officers then shoved, and one unintentionally shoved Bessie. The impact of her hand against his face terminated the phoney period of this war.

Although four against fifty, the invaders performed magnificently. They were all hard and large and proficient in the art of Australian warfare, but sheer poundage submerged them. The mighty Red Kelly, in his namesake's steel armour, found himself at too great a disadvantage, and he removed his helmet and jammed it over the head of the man with the revolver. With his comrades he was forced back and back to the door;

his arm was almost broken in an attempt to make him release his hold on the weapon which was passed to Red Kelly.

Red pushed aside a fellow Irishman the better to take aim at the leader of the excise men, and then found Bony on his back, bending his head forward the better to reach the gun, or least to deflect the aim. Bony, however, was unable to obtain proper purchase of Red with his legs because of the armour, and Red fired before he could be mastered. He missed and concentrated his attention on his clawing attacker, bending and heaving and screaming unintelligible threats.

If the leather thongs tying together the back and front plates had not broken, he would not have dislodged Bony. When they did, Bony and the armour slid off Red to the floor and became one with the pounding feet. He was kicked and cuffed and trodden upon, and on effecting an escape found himself on the outside of the mêlée . . . with the revolver.

Then he observed an extraoreinary sight. Old Gaffer was dancing on the counter, a bottle of a well-known brand of whisky in one hand and his breeches in the other. A knot of women spectators were near the rear door, and the tenor was on the stage, singing without accompaniment 'Black is the Colour'.

Bony could see Red Kelly's head above the mass, but Red being in the middle of the press was unable to get his hands up, and was yelling for a space to 'kill the bliddy bastids'. There was nothing Bony could do, except to pull the fallen from under the mass.

He found Bessie assisting him and wondered how she had managed to escape. Bessie was screaming with excitement. Half her clothes were torn away, and soon it was apparent that her objective was less the preservation of life than something in the centre of the mass. Joe Flanagan and another man were rescued unconscious. Jack the Smuggler and two others were alive and rushed back into the fray. And the tenor changed his song to 'Did Your Mother Come From Ireland'.

Shocked, bleeding from the nose and with a gash somewhere in his scalp, Bony stood back and experienced resignation. He was sure that when this fight was over at least one man would be dead, and many others fit for hospital. He could no longer see Red Kelly.

Brian Kelly left his wall. He put on his helmet. For a moment or two he swayed on his thick legs before taking up a chair. With his right hand he pulled, and with his left he pushed. The chair came apart, and the wrecker now had a shillelagh in each hand. He reminded Bony of the piper when, with abrupt control, he advanced to the rear of the seething mass and without observable malice aforethought, proceeded to tap the combatants one by one.

The effect was an Irishry. The reduction of pressure on the outside produced an explosive effect in the centre. Red Kelly reappeared, the mighty man of black hair and whiskers and a mass of red hair on his naked chest. Men fell upon his son, and left a wide clear passage from Red to Bony.

What Red said Bony could not hear, but he could see Red's intention expressed by the small blue eyes and crouching attitude. He retreated to extend the distance between them, knowing that this man was incapable of learning from experience, and feeling a tinge of pity for such a fine human animal bereft of normal intelligence.

The noise subsided. Jack the Smuggler shouted:

"Not that way, Red. Not that way."

But Red Kelly was launched. He sped across the intervening yards, hands thrust forward to grasp, his brain anticipating, his eyes aflame with lust. He stepped into Bony's hands, and became his own springboard.

He rose, and in that instant must have understood he was bankrupt of all profit from experience. He bent his head forward on the way up and thus his enormous shoulders met the ceiling. He would have made a fairly clean hole through the plaster between the joists, but unfortunately his shoulders up-thrusted a joist, which, because of age, snapped and loosened a cross-joist. He came down again, followed by more than half the entire ceiling.

Pandemonium was revived. The dust of a century mingled with the dust of the plaster and became the universal pacifier. Red opened his mouth to shout and his lungs were filled with dust. Men crouched in paroxysms of coughing. Gaffer seemed to be in a vacuum and continued his dervish dancing on the counter, and Bony stood in another vacuum on the stage beside the singer, who was still singing. And on to the battlefield marched the police.

Sergeant O'Leary was a good tactician, and his army was fourteen-man strong. He broke the combatants into sections, making Red Kelly a section by himself. He had old Gaffer down off the counter. He ordered the handcuffing of Red Kelly for continuing to be violent. The near dead were examined and persuaded to stand or sit, and beyond the settling dust Bony could, thankfully, see no dead men.

"Why are you people interfering?"

Sergeant O'Leary found Bony confronting him.

"Seems to have been a mix up, Inspector," he said, and hastened to add: "Don't mean here. We were informed that customs intended barging in, and were instructed to preserve our rights, as it were."

"The terms of my assignment were clear," snapped Bony.

"Still yours, sir," agreed O'Leary, trying hard to prevent a coughing fit.

"Thanks. First I'll deal with these customs people." He confronted the four intruders, no less ludicrously disarrayed than they. "I am Inspector Bonaparte, in charge here. You will leave at once."

"Like hell we will," growled the leader.

"Then you will be arrested and charged with riotous behaviour, being unlawfully on enclosed premises, and wilfully damaging private property. The choice is yours."

Bony gambled on there being no warrant, and won. The leader glanced upward at where the ceiling had been, shrugged and led his men away. The sergeant was smiling grimly. He foresaw much departmental strife, but in him *esprit de corps* was strong. Bony beckoned forward the men holding Red Kelly.

"Red, I am finding myself reluctant to do what I have to do. This night you have committed the same mistake made by Ned Kelly at Glenrowan. You permitted a few drinks to cloud your mind. The boy gave you warning, and you ignored it. You have brought much trouble to the people of Cork Valley, through that mistake. And I now arrest you for the murder of Eric Torby, alias Hillier. Anything you say may be taken down and used against you." Then Bony shouted, astonishing O'Leary: "SO SHUT UP!"

CHAPTER 26

The Prodigal Conway

THE NIGHT was wild with wind and scattering rain, and now and then faint whirls of blue smoke were puffed into the living-room where Grandma Conway sat gazing with cold sadness at the burning logs. With her was her grandson, and his wife was about to dish up the dinner. Talking softly in a distant corner were Joe Flanagan and Steve the Smuggler. It was the second night following the Ned Kelly Festival.

"Will they hang Red?" asked Grandma, not looking at Mike.

"You've asked that before," he said. "They don't hang in New South Wales. He'll probably get twelve years and be let out in eight if he behaves himself."

"He won't behave, Mike. Doesn't know how to. What did Brian come to see you about?"

"Not about Red. He said he'd spoken to Rosalie about marriage yesterday. He told her that he could make something of his life with his father out of the way, and asked her to wait for him to give proof of it. What he wants us to do is not to insist that he makes the trip to Ireland. I've spoken to Rosalie, and she told me she'd want a year to make up her mind."

"Then let 'em bide, Mike."

"Best policy, I think."

"Yes, let 'em bide. We have troubles enough right now."

Mike sighed. "If only I hadn't picked up that feller."

"Don't be blamin' of yourself, Mike. He took us all in. He even took me in, what with . . . what with . . . "

The old lady stiffened, looked up into her grandson's face.

From outside the room there came to them the leaf rendering of 'Danny Boy'. Mike stood. Mate froze in the act of opening the oven door. The tune became louder, and now they knew it came from the back door. Then Bony appeared. The

189

wind had flailed his hair, and above the cupped hands, holding the leaf against his lips, his eyes were bright and very blue.

The two men at the end of the room advanced swiftly, and Mike waved them back. He himself stepped backward while continuing to face Bony who came to a halt before Grandma. The used leaf was tossed into the fire, and he said:

"Being a Conway I've come to relieve your minds of little worries, and bid you all farewell before going home to my wife and sons near Brisbane."

"You're no Conway," Mike said, icily, his eyes blazing.

"Oh, but I am, and proud of it, too. You remember when you and Red and I found where the bushwalkers came down to the valley. From what Red said as we stood there, I knew you had nothing to do with Torby's murder, and that you fully believed he was alive. The letter you received and which you believed came from him was actually written by O'Halloran and posted in Sydney.

"I've had a conversation with Red in the cell. D'you know why he did it? How many times has he said: 'I believe in being carshious'? He hit Brian and got him from the car. He drove off with Torby to a quiet place, and broke his neck, and then waited till early morning to dump the body on the road to Bowral, after removing the clothes and dressing it in working-clothes. He was burning the clothes and rucksack in the kitchen stove when the cook got up that morning.

"I explained to Red what all that was going to mean to everyone here in Cork Valley, how all of you could be in serious trouble over the back-door trading. I impressed on him that a number of you could be imprisoned for making Mountain Dew, and afterwards have the excise officers always on your backs."

"They haven't come. We've been expecting them. Do you know why?" Mike asked.

"I believe I do. I was given the job of investigating the death of Torby, and the condition I laid down when taking it was that there would be no police interference with me. Those bushwalkers worried me, so I sent a message to Torby's address, confident it would be handed to the police. Instead it was passed to the customs people, and, as you know, they jumped the gun. You will agree that if O'Leary hadn't appeared, the end of the festival might have been really electric.

"There is then the death of a man named Kelso," continued Bony sternly. "I was relieved to know that no one of Cork Valley was involved save Red, and that the affair occurred more than a hundred miles south of Cork Valley. The degree of Red's participation in that crime has yet to be investigated and I don't think you will be concerned. In order to avoid innocent persons being involved in Red's crimes, I persuaded him to admit that he killed Torby for a reason entirely his own, which is the truth, and although he isn't highly intelligent I believe he will stand by it in his loyalty to Cork Valley."

They were silent for several moments before Mike questioned.

"And what will you be doing?"

"I shall prepare the case against him. Is there something else?"

"You know about the still? Red told you?" Grandma asserted.

"As though Red would," Bony said reproachfully. "That's a lovely still an' all; and what pearly Mountain Dew!" Bony took them both into his faint smile. "I'm going to ask you a favour. Destroy that still and terminate the back-door trading. Will you do so?"

"And supposin' we couldn't have the heart to, Inspector Dinkum-Irish Bonaparte?" answered Grandma.

"Then I would be leaving you with a sad heart, and would regret that you made me a Conway."

"Would ye be after denying us our rights?" she persisted, eyes bright, colour high in her china-like cheeks.

"I'm not, Grandma, but the customs will be. Remember times have changed. We ordinary people haven't any rights but to obey what has been made legal. And look you here. Some time or other you could make a teeny-weeny still just to provide a taste or two at the next Ned Kelly Festival. But no back-door trading."

Joe and Steve were standing behind Grandma's chair. Rosalie stood behind them, Bessie O'Grady's arm about her waist. Grandma Conway said: "Nat, me bhoy, I cannot say nay to ye."

"It'll be right, Nat. We'll destroy the still first thing in the morning," seconded Mike.

"And will you send me an invitation to the next festival?"

"Being a Conway, Nat, being a Conway," Grandma instantly agreed, and Mike asked:

"Would you tell us how the customs and police got down here on such short notice to us?"

"Of course. They entered the valley down the cliffs by means of ropes and ladders. They planned the way when they finally understood they could never hope to spring a raid by following the normal route. The police came down by the same way, having trailed the excise officers, and they chose a new route when they found out that the way Torby came in had been wrecked with explosive.

"As I mentioned, conditions have altered. The long era of free enterprise has ended." Bony broke into his stage Irish. "I thank 'e in advance for askin' of me to come to the Ned Kelly Festival next year, and now, before I jine ye at table I'll be a-serenadin' of ye, Grandma. What'll it be?"

She spoke in Gaelic, and Mate Conway exclaimed:

"Speak English, Grandma."

"To the divil with English," Bony said, producing a gum leaf. "I know the Gaelic for 'Danny Boy'."